James Greenwood

Humphrey Dyot

Vol. 2

SALZWASSER
VERLAG

James Greenwood

Humphrey Dyot

Vol. 2

1st Edition | ISBN: 978-3-75256-415-0

Place of Publication: Frankfurt am Main, Germany

Year of Publication: 2022

Salzwasser Verlag GmbH, Germany.

Reprint of the original, first published in 1867.

HUMPHREY DYOT.

HUMPHREY DYOT.

A Novel.

BY

JAMES GREENWOOD,

AUTHOR OF "A NIGHT IN A WORKHOUSE."

IN THREE VOLUMES.

VOL. II.

LONDON:
SAMPSON LOW, SON, AND MARSTON,
MILTON HOUSE, LUDGATE HILL.
MDCCCLXVII.

CONTENTS.

CHAPTER I.

CHAPTER II.

CHAPTER III.

CHAPTER IV.

CHAPTER V.

CHAPTER VI.

CHAPTER VII.

CHAPTER VIII.

CHAPTER IX.

CHAPTER X.

CHAPTER XI.

CHAPTER XII.

CHAPTER XIII.

CHAPTER XIV.

CHAPTER XV.

CHAPTER XVI.

CHAPTER XVII.

CHAPTER XVIII.

CHAPTER XIX.

HUMPHREY DYOT.

CHAPTER I.

MARY IS PROMOTED TO THE DIGNITY OF LITERARY CRITIC.

The white face of Humphrey Dyot haunted Mary continually. It was a painful face, that told of secret suffering, but as free from cunning or dishonest expression as a child's; and she thought so the more now that, in her perplexity, she took frequent note of it.

Perhaps Humphrey discovered that he was the object of the little drudge's solicitous observation; and, conscious of his wan visage, was thankful for her disinterested sympathy, and took pains when he had occasion to speak with her, to do so with even more than his accustomed kindliness. And so they grew to be quite friends, in a sort of way; the oddest part of it being —in Humphrey's eyes, that is—that with the increase of their small friendship, Mary's manner became more shy and inexplicable.

"She looks as though she wished to consult with me on some subject, and was afraid," mused Humphrey. "Perhaps, poor girl, she is quite without friends, and is distressed for some advice that she thinks I may be able to give her. I am afraid that she is not very comfortable here; and that is a pity, for she has a simple, honest face, and is a pretty child, and very intelligent. Does she pray that she may not be led into temptation, I wonder? If so, then I will add my prayers to hers. If she does not, then there is the more reason why she should be prayed for."

And there and then the solitary man knelt down and prayed for Mary's sake, earnestly as though he had been her father, or, at the least, her appointed pastor.

And I am the more glad to tell of this

act of Christian generosity of Mr. Dyot, because, as a mere scribe and recorder of events, it is my duty to narrate that from this time his thoughts dwelt on Mary Kettering very considerably, and that when he by accident encountered her his looks were even shyer and more embarrassed than were hers; and if ever a man looked as though he had something to communicate, but lacked the courage to put his design into practice, that man was Humphrey Dyot.

Had Mary Kettering been a guest of Miss Gurd, and Mr. Dyot as blooming and sprightly, as was quite possible to a man of his years, a person of but small experience in such matters would have had but little hesitation in expressing an opinion that sweethearting was in the wind; but as the matter stood as regards the lady, her sad heart was none too big to contain her bitter sorrow for her lost baby; and as for the gentleman, he was a grave and solemn personage for whom even the vainest of human vanities had not the least attraction.

On one occasion it really seemed to Mary that he was about to open his mouth for the relief of his mind. She had been sent to the stationer's to fetch him some pens, and when she carried them up to his room, instead of meeting her at the door, as was his custom, when she knocked at it, he called "Come in!" So she went in, and found him sitting at his writing-table.

"Thank you, Mary; you look tired," said he.

"I am not very tired, sir," she replied, looking much more confused than his common-place remark warranted, as she backed to the door. "I am accustomed to active employment."

"You are very young to undertake the work of a house," said Mr. Dyot; "and you don't look as though you were trained to hard work."

"Perhaps I look younger than I am, sir," answered Mary, speaking as though her thoughts were with her action rather than with her speech Looking very bashful and confused, her hand sought the little pocket in her gown.

"But you are quite a child," persisted Mr. Dyot.

"I am in my twenty-first year, sir,"

replied Mary Kettering. "I hope that you——"

"Will excuse the liberty," were the words meant to follow, and which, together with a few other words, well weighed and considered, were meant to preface the withdrawing from the little gown-pocket the something that Mary had been so nervously fidgeting to find; but Mr. Dyot cut her short.

"Indeed! Are you as old as that?" he exclaimed, in tones of surprise and disappointment. "I did not think that you were nearly so old. That will do; thank you." And with that he spread out his papers before him, and bent to his work in unmistakable intimation that the conference was at an end, so that Mary could do no other than withdraw from the room, biting her lip in vexation as she did so, and looking almost as disappointed as did he.

From the very beginning of this story, it has been the author's aim to set aside, to the very best of his means and when it is in his power (which it is not invariably, as the good reader will please understand), any manner of mystery that may arise to dim the outlook. He hastens to do so on this occasion.

First of all, as to Mr. Dyot's strange behaviour. He was in grave difficulty, poor man; arising out of the pursuit of that foreign religion of his, and with the nature of which the reader has been already made acquainted. His debtor and creditor account did not progress at all to his satisfaction. It was bad enough—too bad by many and many a woful entry—while he confined his book-keeping to the current thoughts and events of his life; but with this he had grown dissatisfied, and nothing would pacify his accusing conscience but that he must turn back the leaves of his memory, and transcribe therefrom to the pages of his life's ledger the countless shamefulness there recorded. It was an undertaking tremendous and appalling. It was nothing less than conjuring up hosts of ugly ghosts, and embodying them and making them act their mad and wicked antics over again. Nor would the ghosts consent to be laid after this rousing from their long repose. The clasping of his ledger could not hold them in bond, nor the locking of the curiously-clever lock of the iron tomb to which, when not in use, the Doomsday-book was consigned. They haunted him from his rising in the morning till his lying down, and they cried out to him in the still night. They were his children, and would not be denied. They refused to be prayed away, groaned away, cried away; he had whistled them up from the grave, where they had been charitably bestowed, and, being possibly dubious as to finding their way back, they stuck to their father.

As for him, deluded man! he was confounded and bewildered, and lacked courage to call up any more ghosts of the past, although, now that the colony was disturbed, they all found voice, and clamoured at the gate of his memory to be let loose. Was it possible that he could be responsible for such a multitude of sins? Was ever man so frightfully wicked? Would any human being, reading this story of his life, believe that such a monster ever had existence? These, and kindred thoughts, made him shudder as he hid his face in his hands.

There was this to be considered, however. It was possible that, being himself the author of all this iniquity, and knowing the details of it which, with all his desperate courage, he never dare set down, he exaggerated its heinousness. Would he could put the possibility to the test! But it were absurd to waste a thought on the idea of or how by any manœuvring it could be realized.

Yes, there was one way of accomplishing it. He might transcribe certain passages from his record—some of the worst on the wrong side and some of what appeared the best on the creditor side by way of balance, and obtain somebody's opinion on them—somebody who should be led to suppose that there was no reality in the written account, but that it was merely a fictitious story such as any romance-writer might invent. To be sure, to convey this false impression it would be necessary to tell a lie; but that, if a night of prayer might atone for it, were cheaply risked in such a service. Who could he ask? Gurd and his sister were his only intimates; but——well, to tell the truth, of late grave misgivings as to the sincerity of the friendship of these good folks for him had crept into his mind, and he could not ask them. Besides, if no other obstacle had presented, he should prefer that some one less experienced in the ways of the world than the worthy brother and sister should be his judge. A young mind would be more likely to do him justice—that is, the sort of "justice" he wanted: a justice that would treat him pityingly and generously, and chastise him, if needful, with the flat of her sword rather than cleave him with its keen and rigid edge.

While this fantastic desire was troubling his brain, that which has been already related set him thinking of Mary Kettering, till at last he convinced himself that he could do no better than, if possible, engage her in the momentous business that he was bent on. Regarding her out of his sad, prematurely grey-grown eyes, he had settled in his mind that Mary was more youthful than she really was; and, finding that she had attained the womanly age of twenty-one, it a little frightened him from his design. But he returned to it, as will presently be seen.

Then as to the cause of Mary Kettering's embarrassment and disappointment. This may be told in much fewer words than were necessary to put the explanation of Mr. Dyot's case before the reader.

After much deliberation and communing in secret she had resolved on the step she would take towards making the poor gentleman acquainted with her suspicions as to the sort of people they were into whose hands he had fallen. She would trust Mr. Dyot so far as to place in his hands Miss Mercy's "notes," leaving him to act on them as seemed best to him. This resolution, however, came long before an opportunity of putting it into practice, and she had carried Mrs. Craven's letter in the little pocket of her gown three days and over when the chance of delivering it occurred, as already narrated—the chance that was nipped in the bud so unceremoniously by Mr. Dyot himself.

"How should my age concern him?" wondered Mary Kettering. "Why was he disappointed at finding me older than he imagined? Such a remark from some men might be set down as mere silly flattery;

but he is not of the sort that flatter: he really meant it, and was sorry to find himself mistaken. Why, I wonder, was he sorry?"

And Mary's wonder was of two long days' duration, by which time it had grown so prodigiously that she could not comfortably contain it. On the afternoon of the third day, however, the pitying fates vouchsafed her relief. Since the memorable interview, she had not so much as seen Humphrey, Miss Gurd having of late taken on herself the entire care and responsibility of attending on her ailing lodger, but on the occasion in question she was away from home—a fact which Mr. Dyot was possibly made aware of, since Mercy appeared to regard it as her privilege, as mistress of the house, to slam the street-door with a most imposing sound whenever it was her ladyship's pleasure to walk abroad.

In answer to the ringing of Mr. Humphrey Dyot's bell, Mary went up, and was called in as before. As on the previous occasion, he was seated at his table, which was strewn with writing materials, and before him lay a little folded packet of manuscript. His face flushed red as Mary made her appearance, and then fell pale again, paler even than in ordinary.

"Did you ring, sir?"

"Yes, Mary. I wish to speak with you on a subject which, although of small moment in itself, is—is of—ahem! considerable importance to me."

This was a formidable beginning, truly; and made none the less so by the circumstance of the speaker's visible emotion, his unsteady voice, and the trembling of his fingers as they fidgeted with the papers lying on the table. It was very like as if the poor gentleman's eccentricity was about to take the more serious shape of absolute insanity. It was calm, inoffensive madness, however.

"Yes sir," said Mary.

"It will not astonish me if you decline to entertain the proposition I am about to make to you," continued the poor gentleman, resolutely fixing his eyes on the inkstand, so as to avoid Mary's amazed face. "Perhaps you will show more wisdom in declining than I do in hazarding the suggestion. At the worst, however, I trust that you will not misjudge my freedom."

Tantalizing in the extreme was this polite rigmarole. "I was very busy downstairs when you rang your bell, sir," Mary hinted.

"Exactly; I will not detain you many minutes, my good girl," resumed the poor gentleman, nervously. "In the first place, however, Mary, I must apologise to you for my apparent rudeness of last Tuesday."

"I do not remember, sir," Mary answered, which was very like a fib. She *did* remember, and could have repeated every word of the rudeness to which Mr. Dyot alluded.

"You are very kind to say so," returned he. "It was not intended as a rudeness, however, I give you my word of honour. When I told you that I thought that you were younger than you afterwards told me that you were, I was really surprised, and, I may say, a little disappointed. I had private reasons for my disappointment, Mary, as you shall presently hear. And now we will get to business straight.

I wish to be permitted to confide a secret to you, Mary."

"A secret! To me, sir?" It was no make-believe astonishment that opened Mary Kettering's eyes so wide. "I think, sir, that I am scarcely a fit person——"

"A fit person for my purpose, if you will pardon me interrupting you," said Mr. Dyot, "is an intelligent and kindly person, and that you are both these I make no question. Hear my proposition to its end, my good girl, before you reject it. I beseech you to do so. I think I need not ask you can you read, Mary?"

"I can, sir," Mary answered, quietly.

"I don't mean print merely; you can read fair writing?"

"I was several years at school, sir."

"Precisely. That was settled in my mind before I asked you."

Then there was awkward pause, during which Mr. Dyot hung his head, and meddled with his papers, though, evidently, his only object was to conceal his embarrassment.

"Really, simple as the matter is, I am at a loss for words in which to describe it to you," he remarked, suddenly looking up. "Do you ever read stories, Mary?"

"Stories, sir?"

"Ay; novels, romances—fictitious records of human experience, and thankless painstaking and folly. Young women commonly indulge in that kind of pastime, I believe."

Had Mary read novels? Ay, many a score of them. In the old sunny times baby's father used to procure them for her at the library where his mamma dealt, setting them down to that lady's account. Before she had personal occasion for her tears (the demand exceeded the supply afterwards) many a bright afternoon, sitting at her window that overlooked the great Kensington garden, had she shed them copiously over the wrongs and betrayals of injured innocence in three volumes. She was not so far candid with Mr. Dyot; but freely enough she confessed her acquaintance with fictitious literature, wondering more and more to what end the poor gentleman's questions were tending, you may be sure.

"All manner of stories, I presume?

Stories of men's lives, and struggles, and temptations, and failings, and triumphs, amongst the number?"

"Very possibly."

"Stories of vain aspirings, of mistaken ambitions, and the inevitable fall and humiliation resulting."

"I dare say," returned Mary.

"That's well," replied Mr. Humphrey Dyot, emphatically; and then, with that painful attempt at smiling that was sadder to contemplate than the saddest gravity, he continued,

"I suppose that I may take it for granted that it was never your misfortune to make the acquaintance of an author—of an inventor and writer of these works of fiction?"

Mary shook her head, wishing that the interview was at an end.

"You see one before you, my good girl. I am a writer of—of works of fiction. I am an author, a story-writer, Mary; and now that the ice is so far broken, possibly we may get along better."

Without doubt, he *was* an eccentric gentleman.

"I won't detain you a minute longer, Mary. Here are the brief facts of the case [now he spoke with great rapidity]. I am engaged in writing a fanciful history of a man's life—quite a fanciful history, you must understand. It is supposed to take the form of a diary. I don't pretend to any originality in the—the idea; but I think that I have delved deeper into it than any man yet did. In fact, my good girl [here that ghastly smile that gave his white lips an opportunity for contrasting as to colour with his teeth], I begin to think that I have painted my poor wretch so monstrously wicked that folks who read about him will cast my—my book aside as a caricature too diabolical and repulsive. You who have read stories—stories of men's lives, with their temptations, and struggles, and the many, many pitfalls dug in their path—must see how easily this may happen?"

The poor gentleman spoke with so much eagerness and earnestness that it seemed too bad to put him off with merely a monosyllabic answer.

"I don't know much about such matters," Mary remarked; "but it seems to me that it would be difficult for one man to imagine a wickedness that some other man would not be capable of performing. It only requires a person to be as wicked as the author of evil can make him, and—as one is led to believe that there are many such—and there, sir, you have one whose sinfulness it would be impossible to exaggerate."

Mary blushed considerably after this little speech, and the colour did not retreat a bit the faster—nay, was rather fascinated and held in her face—by the startled and painful look the poor gentleman gave her as she ceased speaking. It was the sort of look with which an unlucky criminal regards the judge when, in the course of his "summing up," his lordship holds up in view of the jury a bit of evidence which demands the culprit's condemnation.

"To be sure, to be sure," he presently remarked, withdrawing his gaze and shuffling aimlessly with his papers; "as you very sensibly observed, in such a case it would be impossible to—to paint a poor wretch in colours too black. You must understand, Mary, that this story-writing is quite a secret of mine; never before have I spoken to any one person concerning it."

"And what may be your object in confiding it to me, sir?" Mary asked.

"I will tell you; and the more willingly that you have shown yourself capable, beyond my expectation, of serving me, if you will. What I stand in need of is the deliberate judgment of a fresh and impartial mind on the behaviour of this—this unfortunate wretch of mine. It may seem a strange thing to ask of you; but I am an outcast and solitary man, and driven to great straits for a friend. So I come a-begging to you, little Mary."

"I am sure that I am willing to be of assistance to you, sir, in any way that I may," spoke Mary Kettering, whose heart was touched, as it well might have been, at the mournful tone in which the poor gentleman spoke of his friendlessness. "What is it that you would wish me to do?"

"To keep this secret of mine, first of all, my good Mary," said Mr. Dyot, brightening up a bit. "This secret of the story-writing, I mean."

"That, at least, I promise, sir," Mary answered.

"And for the rest," continued the poor gentleman, "will you be so kind as to take this little batch of manuscript—I have been at great pains to write it very plainly—and at your leisure read it, and frankly give me your opinion on it? I may tell you that you will find little or nothing of the actual story in what I place in your hands; what I have done is to select a few passages—extracts from the diary, let us call them—such as, for the reasons I have already explained, I am most in doubt about. Will you do this for me?"

"I am afraid it will be little to your advantage, sir," Mary replied, smilingly; "I should be found handier at cookery than criticism; but I am willing to do as you desire, if it will gratify you. You must be content, however, to take my opinion without questioning the grounds of it."

"I ask no more, Mary," replied the poor gentleman, gratefully, as he placed the little packet of manuscript in her hands.

"And if I should find no opportunity to tell you verbally what my opinion is, I will write it down on the back of one of the pages."

"That will do excellently."

And so Mary, promoted from kitchen-maid to the dignity of literary critic, took the MS. and carried it straight to her room and locked it in her box till bed-time. By this time she had lost all her scruples as to the propriety of humouring him in his whim. Poor fellow! He was mad, without doubt. One of those harmless lunatics whose delusion is that they have some tremendous talent for this or that, but which, for reasons best known to their insane selves, they conceal and make a profound secret of.

Such were Mary Kettering's thoughts on the matter; and there is little doubt that, had she been on friendly terms with her mistress, she would have told her all about her interview with the poor gentleman and his queer request as soon as she came home. As for the "notes" that were originally intended for Mr. Dyot, the paper on which they were inscribed still remained in her pocket. Let them be never so harmless, in his mania for plotting and story-writing he would be sure to find mischief in them.

Nevertheless, come bed-time, Mary could no longer defer her curiosity to taste the quality of Mr. Dyot's literary production. "It is as mad as his talk, no doubt," said she; "and the shortest way would be to write on the packet 'beyond my comprehension,' and return it unread. But I promised him that I would read it; besides, a story of horror and unheard-of wickedness is fit to be read in such a cheerful, well-lit chamber as this is." And she shrugged her shoulders as she looked round on the stained and patched lime-washed wall and ceiling, and on the rickety window-sash, and the slender, ghostly rushlight, that stared at her with its solitary, bleary eye of red and yellow.

As the poor gentleman had given her to understand, there was nothing of the roundness of a perfect story in the manuscript: indeed, it was almost as difficult to judge of its entire shape and make as of the shape of a cake by a few stray crumbs of it.

Before she had perused six pages of the writing, Mary Kettering began to suspect the truth—that the "story-writer's" hero was no other than the story-writer himself. It was seldom that the "leading character" was spoken of by name, and then he was called "Bertram," such being the cunning little alteration the poor gentleman had made in transcribing these examples of his thoughts and experiences from his ledger. But, unfortunately for his case, the peculiar mannerism that distinguished him gave complexion alike to his speaking and his writing, and even his looks and gestures, so that, having once conversed with him, you heard him speak as you read his writing, and you knew that it was of Dyot of whom the revelation was, and not Bertram.

For "mannerism," however, Mary Kettering substituted "madness." "No man but one inclined to madness could have been guilty of so wicked an existence; no one but a downright madman, driven beyond his reason by depravity, could bring himself to sit down and inscribe the story of his own infamy secretly, and, as it seemed, for no other end than his amusement."

This was Mary's opinion when she had read no more than six pages of the manuscript; when, however, she had accomplished twice six (and the task was easy enough, the story being beautifully written) her suspicion that Bertram was Mr. Humphrey Dyot was confirmed to certainty. As previously stated, there was nothing like continuity in the extracts from the diary, and the twelfth page began:—

"On the evening of this day, as it seemed to me, my fever grew to its height, when, as I lay in my hammock, my reason playing hide-and-seek in my poor, hot head, I fancied that I heard aboveboard sounds as though the boats were being lowered; a trampling and an unusual commotion; and then all as still as though the ship and crew were suddenly stricken dead. Then, immediately ensuing, came a fit of delirium, and I fancied that it was myself that was dead, and that was why I could not hear any sound. Whether or no my senses were in me when I scrambled out o' bed and made for the deck, I cannot say, but there, to my horror, I beheld——"

Then followed, told in sane and graphic language, a description of what he beheld, and which it is unnecessary here to repeat, since the reader already knows all about it. He described the boats rowing away from the foundering "Reaper," and his mad entreaty for them to return and take him off; of his despair and the long spell of insensibility that ensued. "Coming out of which," said he, "exhausted and chilled to the marrow of my bones, I very thankfully availed myself of an excellent warm jacket one of the crew had left behind, and in one of the pockets, by good luck, there was a flask of brandy."

Not a word about jewels, not so much as a hint about anything else that he found in the pockets of the jacket. Indeed, no further mention of that garment at all; the remainder of the extract being devoted to self-accusing and reviling due to the narrator because of his monstrous blasphemy at being so cruelly deserted, and his wicked prayers for death.

There was nothing remarkable in this, however. To be sure, Mr. Dyot had placed the extracts in her hands, never dreaming that she was in possession of any previous clue to his history; and, further, that he had been at some pains to destroy his identification in the matter; still, mad or sane, it was extremely unlikely that he would jeopardise his great secret by alluding to it unnecessarily. And with no further comment, Mary continued her perusal of the pages, which were as mad as ever, to the last.

Now for her opinion as literary critic. Was indulgence in this absurd and unjust diary-keeping likely to aggravate the poor gentleman's ailment? It must be so. He had evidently made it his hobby for some considerable time, and undoubtedly he was daily growing more restless and strange in his manner. It would be a charitable thing to dissuade him from a continuation of the hurtful work. So impressed, Mary indorsed the outer leaf of the manuscript as follows:—

"I have read the pages, and to my poor judgment, Bertram is an impossible being. Even supposing the existence of so terribly wicked a creature, his life, if this may be taken as a sample of it, is a thing to be forgotten rather than published to the world."

Not the next day, however, nor the day following, did she find opportunity to return the poor gentleman his manuscript. Whether there were grounds for the suspicion need not be here considered, but it seemed to Mary that her mistress was, during the last day or two, particularly anxious that she should in no way communicate with the solitary tenant of the back room. The brother and sister seemed to have discovered sudden reason for being strangely apprehensive on the poor gentleman's account.

Keeping her ears open, Mary Kettering repeatedly overheard scraps of alarmed conversation occurring between Anthony and Miss Mercy. Stranger still, the poor gentleman took suddenly to going out, though only for short spells. He would do so several times in a day, and always of a morning and evening, letting himself in quietly with his latch-key.

Another circumstance Mary remarked —for three mornings past Mercy had not carried him his morning coffee.

"Pshaw! There is no need for making it out blacker than it is," grumbled Anthony. "A fortnight is a considerable time. Who knows what may turn up in a fortnight?"

"We may not know what will turn up within that time, but we know who will turn out, and that's quite enough for us," returned Miss Mercy, grimly.

It was on the third day after her interview with the poor gentleman that Mary Kettering overheard this strange scrap of conversation, and the next day happened a chance for her to return Mr. Dyot his literary property.

She tapped lightly at his door, and, he opening it, she put the little packet in his hands, and would then have turned away, had he not eagerly caught her by the sleeve, and so held her while he read what she had written on the outer page. As he did so his sad face assumed an expression that caused Mary instantly to repent her bold criticism.

"And this is fairly your opinion, Mary?" he observed, gently.

"It is so small a one that it is scarcely worth considering, sir," replied she.

"It is fair, and it is true—quite true,

Mary—no doubt of it," said the poor gentleman, with ghastly gaiety. "However, we will make short work of this villanous Bertram. He is to be exterminated, Mary —poisoned like a rat in his hole."

And, so saying, the poor gentleman softly closed the door, leaving Mary to guess his riddle.

CHAPTER II.

THE POOR GENTLEMAN FALLS OUT WITH HIS BREAKFAST, AND ANTHONY, UNSUCCESSFUL WITH THE BOWL, MEDITATES THE DAGGER.

About this time it was revealed to the amazed sick man that his health was being tampered with. How he arrived at this conclusion matters little. He may at some time or another have dabbled in experimental chemistry, or, in his wild days he may have reckoned amongst his companions certain communicative young sprigs of the medical profession, and through them become initiated with as much of its mysteries as at least enabled him to distinguish arsenic from Epsom salts, and belladonna from black draught. He detected the poison imp, or so he thought, lurking in his milk-jug, of all places in the world.

He made no great fuss over his startling discovery, however. When his mind was quite settled on the subject he remarked one morning to Miss Mercy, when she appeared, as usual, smirking and smiling, with his breakfast,

"You need not, for the future, trouble to bring me milk with my coffee, Miss Gurd."

Mercy was [setting the tray down as he spoke, and she could not have completed the operation with greater precipitancy had her hand come in contact with the hot urn.

"No milk, sir? Why not?"

"I prefer it without, thank you," replied Mr. Dyot, quietly.

"Very good, sir," a slight twinge of alarm for a moment disturbed the muscles of Miss Gurd's face, but she speedily recovered herself. "It is a matter of taste. We invariably take milk with our coffee. My brother recommends it for weakly appetites."

"Such as mine, for instance," remarked Mr. Dyot, with a peculiar smile.

"Such as yours is, sir! Milk is

reckoned to be very nutritious, when it is pure and wholesome."

Then Mr. Humphrey Dyot looked up suddenly and regarded her with an expression of countenance that at once told her that something serious was amiss.

"Wholesome! Ay, when it is. But don't you know the wicked lengths people will at times go for the sake of what they foolishly regard as extra profit? Don't you know that it is very possible to adulterate milk?"

The poor gentleman kept his eyes steadily fixed on hers as he spoke, and, though she struggled desperately to return his look calmly and indifferently, she failed signally.

Surely there was nothing in Mr. Dyot's simple observation to make an honest woman turn first guiltily red, and then so white and dismayed. What a pity it is that our faces are not as much under control as our thoughts! How many a secret has escaped in an involuntary blush when the will was good to hold it with the grip of a blacksmith?

"No doubt that it is possible to adulterate it when rogues have dealings with it; but you must admit that there are such folks as honest milkmen, Mr. Dyot," said she, lightly. "However, since you prefer to dispense with milk in your coffee, I will take it down again."

"Don't trouble yourself," exclaimed he, laying his hand on the little vessel; "it is not to the sight, but the flavour of it, that I object. Pray, is it the same that you use at your own table?"

"It is poured from the same measure."

"And you discover nothing peculiar in it—nothing that were better omitted?"

"Nothing being added, there is nothing to omit; you are not well, sir, and your taste is at fault;" and, fussing over the tray, Mercy made a bungling effort to conceal her confusion.

"But the milk *is* wholesome? You know it to be wholesome?" he persisted, taking up the little jug and tilting it, and looking curiously into its depths, and then as curiously at Mercy.

"My goodness, yes! Why should we buy anything that is unwholesome either for ourselves or for you?" And now Mercy giggled, and affected to treat the discussion as a jocular one.

"Not for yourselves—that would be absurd; but with me, who am ailing, it may possibly be different. What may be unwholesome for a man in health, it may be desirable to administer to a man who is ill. Am I to understand you in that sense, Miss Gurd?"

"I am glad to find that you are in such excellent spirits, sir," Mercy returned, evasively. "It is quite cheering to see you so bright and pleasant. My brother will be delighted, I am sure."

"I feel better, I am happy to tell you. Thank God! I have been led to take more than ordinary care of myself of late—such care as will astonish, if it will not delight your brother, Miss Gurd, when he is informed of it, or I am greatly mistaken." And all this time he looked hard at her and followed her eyes with his own, shift and dodge as she might.

"I don't understand you, sir," she replied, presently, and endeavouring to make her grin of fury pass as one of pleasantry. "Why will my brother be astonished when he hears of your mending? You don't pay a high compliment to his skill when you express your belief that the result of the simple medicines he prescribes for you will astonish him."

"But I am afraid I have been a disobedient patient," replied Mr. Dyot, still toying with the little milk-jug.

"How disobedient?"

"I have not taken the simple medicine your brother prescribed for me with anything like the regularity he had reason to expect," returned Mr. Dyot, with a short, bitter laugh. "Without presuming to doubt that Mr. Gurd has been prescribing for me according to the merits of my case, without entering into the perplexing question of why he should take such peculiar interest in my health—me, a poor man and a stranger—I have ventured to neglect his simple medicines: *I have tasted none of them during the last three days!*"

Now indeed was Mercy confounded and plunged in dire perplexity. What did he mean by "your brother's *peculiar* interest in my health?" Any way, it was better to put a bold face on the matter.

"If you will be good enough to express yourself in plain terms, I shall be better able to answer you, Mr. Dyot," she said, sharply. "Have you anything to complain of?"

"I find it exceedingly inconvenient to have to go out and buy my own food. I don't complain of it, I am not a man given to complaining. Still you must admit that it is inconvenient," returned he, coolly.

"Buy your own food!" repeated Mercy, in blank astonishment. "You have bought no food for yourself since you have been with us, Mr. Dyot."

"There you are mistaken, madam. I have eaten no food except of my own buying since last Thursday. You must have observed that I have been out much more frequently of late than was my previous habit."

"But, why—*why* are you set against meals of our preparing?" asked Mercy, in a husky voice, and turning to the window she there looked out, so as to avoid his accusing eyes.

"Perhaps, because, as you just now remarked, my taste is at fault," answered

Mr. Dyot, shrugging his lean shoulders. "Any way, I may as well now inform you, Miss Gurd, that I can no longer rest contented here. I am afraid that I have been but a troublesome and profitless lodger to you, and, no doubt, you will be as glad to get rid of me as I shall be to get away. I will relieve you of my tenancy, if you please, within the next fortnight."

This was coming to the point with a vengeance. At all events, there was no fault now to be found with him on the score of vagueness of speech. Profitless! Why, what he had paid them had not so much as covered the cost of his uncooked food. He had been fed like a prince. Delicacies in the shape of fish and fowl had been daily spread before him to tempt his feeble appetite; wines at five shillings the bottle had been placed at his disposal without stint. In the modest hope of a thousand-fold return, shillings and half-crowns had been expended on the poor gentleman almost cheerfully; and now the ungrateful villain talked of a fortnight's notice and decamping, coolly as though he were the most ordinary of lodgers. These reflections, coursing rapidly through Miss Gurd's mind, exasperated her beyond expression.

"I trust, sir," said she, "that you will be able to give my brother some more reasonable explanation of this sudden whim than you favour me with. I hope that you will, sir; I am sure that he will expect it."

Mr. Dyot rose, and, going to a cupboard, took out a bottle about three parts filled with a liquid like curded milk.

"I am undesirous of entering further than I already have into this disagreeable matter," said he; "but should your brother insist on a more explicit explanation, he will find it in this bottle. I may as well strengthen my reason for resolving as I have." Here he withdrew the cork from the bottle, and poured the morning's allowance of milk that Mercy had just brought up with the rest and corked the bottle again. "If this does not furnish satisfactory explanation I have none other to give. Stay; on second thoughts, it may be as well if I keep this up here. You can inform Mr. Gurd of our conversation, and of what I have here reserved; and if he is still anxious for further discussion on the subject, he must take the consequences." So saying, he returned the bottle to the cupboard, and by a polite gesture intimated that he desired to be relieved of Miss Gurd's presence.

That Mr. Anthony was considerably astonished when his sister, pale with rage and alarm, conveyed Mr. Dyot's message to him, the reader will readily conceive. In his red-hot fury he blurted out a little circumstance that he had hitherto kept most carefully hidden from Miss Mercy.

"Hang him! A pretty fellow he is to preach and threaten!" exclaimed Mr. Anthony. "A thief, whose life is a torment to him, owing to his anxiety for his stolen goods. This is a pretty return for all our kindness—for the handsome way in which he has been boarded and waited on, and all for his wretched guinea a week—for the pounds and pounds I have from time to time been fool enough to part with to keep things snug and comfortable for the——"

"What pounds and pounds are you speaking of? What do you mean by from 'time to time'?" interrupted Mercy, fresh alarms seizing her, and suspicion flashing in her grey eyes.

"What do I mean? Why, that ——. But, there, what's the good of talking about that, now? It's all of a piece."

But he wasn't to be let off so easily. He had already said quite enough to enable his sharp sister to guess the rest.

"You never mean to tell me, Anthony," said she, laying a hand on the little man's shoulder; "you never mean to tell me that you've been fool enough to part with more money in *that* quarter?"

"In what quarter?" returned he, doggedly.

"To that—that—what's his name? That rapacious shark who as good as committed highway robbery on you when this fellow Dyot first came to live with us."

"It's 'fool enough' because the chances of the game have suddenly turned against us. You'd have sung to another tune had everything come about as we planned," growled out Anthony, savage with himself for his unlucky slip of the tongue.

"That's no answer," returned Mercy.

"*Have* you been fool enough to fee this vampire since that affair of the pocket-book?"

"Yes, I have. If you want to know why, I tell you because I chose—because I thought it best," exclaimed the convicted Anthony, having nothing but bluster to fall back on.

"And how much more has he bullied you out of?" asked Mercy, quietly.

"Twenty pounds more; that's how much. Four fives."

"Four fives! In four separate sums, I suppose?"

"In four separate sums. How could I help it? You wouldn't have him coming here and making a row, would you? Wasn't it better to shut the scoundrel's mouth with a pound now and then till—till——there, you know well enough what I mean without my saying it."

"A regular pensioner, eh," said Mercy, bitterly; "comes for his hush-money on such a day, as the clock strikes!"

"No; sometimes he sends," Anthony replied, with grim malice, as though it gave him pleasure to give his sister a taste of the scourge she had displayed such diligence in discovering.

"Sends!" almost screamed Miss Mercy.

"Sends his brother—so the blackguard calls himself. A cleverer scoundrel than Mr. Micah by ten times; a cool, easy-going ruffian; and daring as the devil himself."

Mercy's lips fairly quivered with rage. "And what does this clever scoundrel know?" she asked.

"That's where he shows himself so clever," answered Anthony. "I can't tell you what he knows, how much or how little."

"He knows *you*, and he need know no more," laughed Mercy, bitterly. "He knows when he has got hold of a calf who will lick his hand while he bleeds you."

"He has bled me for the last time, however. It will be worth something to tell him so the next time I meet him."

"If you think that Dyot is likely to make any fuss concerning the confounded milk bottle, it will be better to have first pull, at all hazards," remarked the doctor to his sister, when he had grown somewhat cool.

"How do you mean, first pull?" asked Mercy.

"Why, to insist on knowing what he means; to demand immediate explanation of his accusation," replied Mr. Gurd; "that is, if you think it is likely that he will make any move."

"But I think nothing of the kind," replied Mercy. "It doesn't stand to reason that he should make any move. He has taken fright, and will be only too glad to get off with his precious secret without any bother. It is what is in that iron box that shuts his mouth. Would any man who was free to have his affairs discussed, and who has the suspicions he has, let the matter pass over as quietly as he is inclined to?"

"There's blister as well as balm in that," replied Mr. Gurd, grating his teeth. "Of course, it is what is in the iron box that shuts his mouth. I tell you what, if it wasn't for that infernal bottle I'd just walk up straight to him and cry 'Halves!' and take nothing less."

"But, as the case stands, and taking the infernal bottle into consideration?" suggested his sister.

"Why, the risk is greater than the possible gain, and there is no use in making bad worse," returned Anthony. "All I wish is that he may still stay the fortnight. I haven't given up all hope yet, Mercy, if you have. We shall see who is right."

"You haven't been inventing any more of your precious private schemes, have you?" Mercy remarked, anxiously, her suspicions roused by the peculiar stress her brother laid on the concluding words of his last observation. "For Heaven's sake let us work together, Tony, or not at all! You'll hobble us both, if you are not careful. I am sure you will."

And Miss Gurd, who really was very unwell, and feverish, here broke into an unusual flood of tears, much to her brother's distress.

"No, no, Mercy, dear, I have no new scheme; upon my word and honour, I haven't! Don't cry. I promise that I won't do anything at all in the business without first consulting you. There!"

It was fortunate for him that, as he spoke, his sister's tearful eyes were covered with her handkerchief; otherwise, she surely would have detected that in his looks which gave the lie to his asseveration.

The fact is, he had new schemes—schemes bold and desperate. His great difficulty was Mercy. To disclose his intentions to her was out of the question; to put them into practice without her knowledge was equally hopeless. He was in a fix.

But having the d—l's luck and his own, as wicked people say, he was presently unfixed by a means all unexpected. Mercy's indisposition increased; and one morning, though vastly against her inclination, she was compelled to admit her inability to rise from her bed; and though, to comfort her, Anthony assured her that it was nothing more than a bad cold, that would pass over in a day or two, he was not such a dunce at his craft as not to perceive that if she was up and doing at the expiration of a week she might consider herself a fortunate woman.

"How strange!" mused Anthony, after he had paid his sister this visit of condolence—"how strange that she should be confined to her bed on the very day I was most anxious that she should be out of the way! Only six days gone yet! It's a race against time, and I shall beat after all, if I am lucky, now that I have got this unexpected start."

And he desisted from rolling the dough out of which his celebrated pills were made, to snap his fingers like anyone but a man who has a sick sister to grieve for.

CHAPTER III.

MR. GURD MAKES A FRIEND OF AN ENEMY, AND INVITES HIM HOME TO DISCUSS A BUSINESS OF SOME DELICACY.

WITH the air of a man embarking on a business he has resolved on going through with, one evening Mr. Gurd, having put up the shutters of his shop, buttoned on his overcoat, and, noiselessly letting himself out, made his way towards London Bridge, never once pausing or looking about him until he arrived at the middle recess. It was vacant, and, from the impatient expression that for a moment shadowed the little doctor's face, it might be assumed that he was disappointed at finding it so.

"No fear as to his coming, that's one consolation," he muttered to himself, with a confident grin, and then, mounting the stone seat, he turned his back on the wayfaring public and affected deep interest in the Yorkshire boats lying at wharf in the river beneath.

"When you are disengaged, sir," whispered some one presently, and Mr. Gurd, turning sharply about, discovered the individual with whom he had made an appointment to meet at this spot, and who was no other than Mr. Edward Blake, of whom the reader has some slight previous knowledge. As already intimated, Mr. Blake had stood in considerable peril of spending at least a year of his future life in compulsory seclusion; but the thief's proverbial good fortune (he was known amongst his most intimate acquaintances as "Lucky Blake") had not forsaken him; and, after being remanded week by week for three weeks, he was finally discharged from prison for want of sufficient evidence against him.

"You're late, my friend," remarked Mr. Gurd, with such affability in his tone as caused Mr. Blake to look about him suddenly and suspiciously lest a constable friend of the treacherous old gentleman should be close at hand.

"You are early, you mean," returned Mr. Blake; "it wants fully two minutes to the half hour; it isn't often that your watch is too fast. What's up?"

By which brief query Mr. Blake meant "What am I to understand from a fact so singular?" while at the same time he regarded the little doctor with a look that plainly expressed, "Are you acting fair and above board? if not, look out!"

"Well, possibly, that I am rather earlier than usual," returned Mr. Gurd, nervously. "The fact is—the truth is, Mr.-a-What's-yourname—I should like to have a little private conversation with you."

"What about?"

"I'll tell you, if you will walk along with me."

"Let me have the money first; we will think about private conversation afterwards," said Blake; and, actuated by the growing conviction that this bland, hesitating behaviour of the doctor boded him no good, his right hand stole round to the tail pocket of his coat as he spoke. "Look sharp; I'm in a hurry, rather! It is to be ten pounds this time, you understand."

"No; the conversation first, and the money afterwards. Just as you like, however," continued he, hastily, suddenly noting the altered expression of the ruffian's countenance. "Here's your money: ten pounds in gold, and already put up for you, Mr. Blake."

Mr. Blake took the little paper packet, and, without breaking it, slipped it into his pocket.

"Look here, master," said he, in a whisper, as he bent his lips to Mr. Gurd's ear; "is there anything else 'put up' for me? Is this a trap?"

"A trap! Bless the man, no. Why do you ask?"

"I'll tell you why. I don't like your talk to-night; I don't like your looks. Why the —— should you talk oily to me? I'm no friend of yours. You'd like to see me behind a prison grating. It is only natural that you should. I should like to see *you* there if we were to change places. It is time a man kept his weather-eye open when his enemy begins soaping him."

Mr. Gurd forced a little laugh.

"My dear fellow," replied he, "I am not at all surprised at your suspicions; they are no more than natural under the circumstances. But, believe me, you were never so much mistaken in all your life as when you suppose that I am at present actuated by any other than honest and straightforward motives. Come along, we will walk towards my house, if you have no objection."

Towards his house! The very way of all others that the doctor had hitherto most strongly objected to his taking. In fact, the Messrs. Blake had traded on this Mr. Gurd's known objection. "I will not be fleeced in this manner!" he had furiously remonstrated on the very last occasion of his paying hush-money to the waiter's brother; "I will not submit to this villanous highway robbery! I will see you both hanged first." "Very good; I have no interest in transacting our little business on the highway," Mr. Blake had replied; "let us get under cover; let us go to your house." Whereon Mr. Gurd produced the money demanded, and handed it over without another word.

"Let us walk towards my house, if you have no objection," said the little doctor; "we can talk as we go, or we will discuss the matter I wish to consult you on no further till we get within doors—that will be safest, perhaps."

"Within whose doors?" inquired Mr. Blake, in unfeigned astonishment.

"Mine."

"Half a moment. I am rather particular whose doors I place myself within," remarked Mr. Blake. "Before we go any further just answer me one question."

"With pleasure," replied Mr. Gurd, politely; "a dozen if needful."

"What is the business in hand?"

"I can put you in the way of doing the most profitable job you ever undertook in all your life," replied Mr. Gurd, still whispering; "a job that scores of fellows would give their ears to be introduced to. A job that will put you independent of all other jobs as long as you live."

Mr. Blake's quick instinct caught the hint instantly.

"Ah!" said he, "now we begin to understand each other a little better."

"We had better be walking, hadn't we?" suggested Mr. Gurd, who felt that he had broken the ice, and certainly looked as though he had suddenly plunged a leg into the cold water beneath it.

"Decidedly. We won't walk together, though. You be off. I'll be at Old Fish Street as soon as you, I'll wager."

"But you mustn't be there before me," remarked Mr. Gurd, hastily. "Say that you will be there in a quarter of an hour from this time."

"In a quarter of an hour, and you will be at home. Shall I knock or ring?" asked the thief, who now was quite reassured, and evidently anxious to ascertain the particulars of this job of jobs.

"Do neither," replied the doctor, after a moment's reflection; "scrape with your foot over the area railings. I shall understand."

And so they parted. If, however, Mr. Gurd imagined that he was allowed to return home unwatched, he was mistaken. While Teddy and the doctor were holding secret conversation in the recess on the bridge, in the next, towards the Surrey side, sat a man, who, by his dress, might have been a bricklayer's labourer quietly smoking his pipe. Mr. Gurd turned towards the City, and Mr. Blake the other way; the latter hurriedly whispered to the labourer as he passed him,

"See him home, Micah; work your cap."

Which simply meant, "signal with your cap. If he goes straight home and speaks to no one, let your cap rest; but if his behaviour is in any way suspicious, raise your cap from your head, and I shall know." It was a whity-brown cap, and might be seen at a considerable distance.

But Mr. Gurd had no treacherous designs; and, all unsuspicious of the bricklayer's labourer, reached his home without justifying the least disturbance of the man's cap. It was as yet not late—eight o'clock or thereabouts. Mary Kettering opened the door to him.

"How is your mistress?" he asked.

"She has just taken the composing draught, sir; and seems inclined for sleep," Mary replied.

"So that she will not require your attendance for half an hour or so," said Mr. Gurd. "That's lucky. You know the drug-shop in Aldgate, where you were sent the other day, Mary?"

"Yes, sir."

"I wish you would go there for me—it will be a pleasant walk for you this fine evening—and ask them to attend to this order as soon as convenient. You need not hurry. If you are back in half an hour it will do."

And within five minutes of Mary departing on her errand, leaving Mr. Gurd in undisturbed possession of the lower part of the premises, the last mentioned worthy heard the preconcerted signal at the area railings, and, creeping softly up the stairs, he let in Mr. Edward Blake, laying a finger on his lip as he did so, as a caution to that young fellow to tread as lightly as possible.

They went down into the front kitchen, where there was a fire, and Mr. Gurd, having first closed the door and cautiously drawn the curtain over the front window, invited his guest to be seated.

CHAPTER IV.

THE CONVERSATION THAT MARY KETTERING HEARD BETWEEN HER MASTER AND HIS STRANGE "PATIENT."

At the rear of Doctor Gurd's premises was a door that opened on to a narrow court. Except for the convenience of the dustman or the coal-carman, this door was seldom or never used, and was kept locked. It so happened, however, that on the morning of the day in question there had been a delivery of coals at Mr. Gurd's, and Mary, after locking the door, had slipped the key into her pocket. There it remained until the evening, when Anthony requested her to go on an errand to Aldgate, and there, as it opportunely occurred, it was when she returned. "If Miss Mercy is asleep, I may wake her by knocking or ringing at the bell," thought Mary Kettering. "I can let myself in by the back way, without disturbing any one."

And this she did, and, being light of step, with so little noise that she reached the back kitchen without in the least disturbing the conspirators in the front, who were engaged in their delicate conversation. They spoke so low that some few moments elapsed before Mary was aware of it, and then she was not a little startled. It was seldom that Mr. Gurd came down into the kitchen—never without his sister. Yet, without doubt, it was Mr. Gurd's voice that she heard. With whom was he talking? Surely not with Mercy, she was ill in bed. Not Mr. Dyot, for it had not escaped her observation that that gentleman and his landlord were at serious variance. Presently, however, she fancied that she heard Mr. Dyot's name mentioned, and instantly she became highly curious to know who it was that Mr. Gurd was talking with. There was a little window of a single pane, high up in the wall, that looked into the front kitchen; and, standing on a chair, she was able to avail herself of the peeping place.

There she saw Mr. Anthony and Mr. Blake, his companion. It was just at the moment the former was favouring his confederate with a view of the drawing of the key that he had obtained, the reader already knows how. She had no doubt, from the guilty expression of Mr. Gurd's countenance, that mischief was brewing, and so, dismounting from the chair, she laid her ear against the wall to listen.

"What do you think of it?" she heard Mr. Gurd inquire.

"Humph! I've seen this sort of thing attempted before, and I've seen it answer, and I've seen a mull made of trying it. Isn't there nothing safer to work on?"

"Nothing."

"Isn't it possible to get *the* key for a minute or so—just long enough to take a cast of it?"

"Quite impossible. You might as well ask for a few minutes' handling of the safe itself."

"It would not be pleasant to find one's self baulked at the last moment."

"Not the least fear of that, I tell you. I saw the drawing made, and can swear that, line for line, it is true with the original. The difficulty is, who can we get to make it?"

"That's the smallest part of the difficulty. Leave that to me. I may as well take charge of the pattern."

"Just so. I leave it all to you."

Here Mary raised herself for a moment, and saw the stranger fold up the scrap of paper and place it in his pocket.

"The sooner it is done the better," remarked Mr. Gurd.

"Ay, ay; but there are other matters to arrange first. How many are there in it?"

"How many what?"

"How many hands. Do you show in the business? I should say not. Rather have your room than your company, I tell you, candidly; but you know best."

"Do I show? Why, what on earth are you talking about, my good fellow? I am to know nothing at all about it, you of course understand that. If I'm disturbed, I rush down to see what the matter is, and to arrest the robber, d'ye see? Be careful how you get in my way, Mr. Blake, you'll repent it if I once lay a hand on you. He! he!"

"But of course you'll have a preliminary hand in it? We can do nothing without you, you know."

"We!"

"Ay; me and my chum."

"But why let another party into the job? I'm sure that you can manage very well by yourself—a bold, cool-headed, young fellow such as you are. To say nothing of the risk, it is an unnecessary expense; no one will help you without expecting a share of—of what's to be got."

"Not likely! Nevertheless, if it comes off at all, it must be a three-handed job—reckoning you as one; and we must share and share alike."

"That is to say, I am to get no more than a wretched third! There is to be no allowance in my favour as being the planner and originator of the affair. I am to get no more than any low vagabond you may choose to select as a companion. Pshaw! you must be joking." And Mr. Gurd, in a voice quivering with passion, laughed.

"I never was more serious in all my

life," returned Mr. Blake. "You get your thirds because you are the planner and putter up of the job; you are nothing else, remember. And, if you take my advice, my friend, you won't call other people ugly names; they don't sound pretty out of a *gentleman's* mouth."

"Well, well; we won't quarrel over our chickens before they are hatched," remarked Mr. Gurd, in a more pacific voice. "There's enough to satisfy three, I dare say. You must bring your friend, I suppose. Who is it to be—Micah?"

Mr. Blake laughed louder than was prudent. "Is it to be a charity-boy out of the school here?" he asked, derisively. "No, my good sir; it is not to be Micah."

"I'm glad to hear it [Mr. Gurd did not look particularly glad, however]. You and your friend, then, shall do the job; and I will tell you how far I can pave the way to it for you."

And then Mr. Gurd hitched his chair closer to Mr. Blake's chair, and dropped his voice to so low a whisper that, listen attentively as Mary might, she could make out no more than a confused hum of voices.

This lasted for fully ten minutes, during which the listener was tantalized beyond endurance.

At last it occurred to her that she might have a better chance of overhearing how Mr. Gurd meant to "pave the way," if she brought her ear to a level of where the little window was, and she placed a foot on the chair to raise herself. She did so, hurriedly and carelessly, however. The chair slipped aside, and fell over with a noise that caused her to utter a sudden exclamation of terror; and it tended not at all to reassure her when she heard a similar sound emanating from the front kitchen. With a woman's quickness, however, she advanced towards the door, opened it just in time to meet Mr. Anthony, candle in hand, and with a face as white as paper.

"You here?" was all the terrified man could say.

"I had the key of the back gate, and I came in that way, so that my ringing might not disturb mistress, sir," replied Mary Kettering, with wonderful coolness. "The drug-shop in Aldgate was shut up; but the man who lives in the house ——"

"How long have you been home? What was that noise that I heard here just now," interrupted Mr. Gurd.

"I blundered against a chair in the dark, sir. I was just coming into the front kitchen to fetch a light." And, with the most innocent face in the world, she made as though to pass him.

"Here's a light, take one from this; you can't come into the kitchen," spoke Anthony, hastily, placing himself before her. "I—I have a patient there. You may as well go to bed; you won't be wanted again to-night. Good-night!"

Suddenly, however, it occurred to him that it might seem to Mary that she was dismissed with extraordinary haste, so, as she was going up the stairs, he called after her.

"Well, what did Craddocks' people say, after all? You haven't told me."

"That the order shall be attended to to-morrow, sir."

"That will do. And, Mary."

"Yes, sir."

"If your mistress should be awake and call you as you pass her door you—you—

need not say that I have a patient come to see me, else she will worry herself as to why I didn't ask him up in the regular way; and worrying isn't good for her fever, poor thing! You'll promise to do as I ask, won't you, my good girl?"

How could she deny a request made in such pretty terms?

"But if Miss Gurd should ask me if there is *anyone* with you, sir?" said Mary.

"Say—say that you saw no one with me; that won't be telling a story, you know. And, Mary, I intended to have given you half-a-crown last Wednesday, which was my birthday, but it quite slipped my memory. Remind me of it in the morning, will you?"

This, likewise, Mary promised, and was then allowed to go her way. As it happened, Miss Gurd was asleep when the young woman passed her door, and, consequently, she was not called; Mary wished that she had been, so that she might have had an excuse for being about the house a little longer; but, as it was, there was nothing for it but to betake her wondering self to bed.

Anthony found his friend looking not a little alarmed when he returned to the kitchen. It may be stated that, while Mary and her master were engaged in conversation, Mr. Blake had stolen to the closed door and surveyed the young woman through the keyhole.

"I thought you said that there was no chance of our talk being overheard?—that nobody but people sick and a-bed were in the house?" exclaimed Mr. Blake, indignantly.

"So I thought. Confound her! I made sure that I should hear her when she returned."

"But confounding her won't make her forget anything she may have heard," grumbled Mr. Blake. "This comes of dealing with bunglers. I've half a mind to have no more to do with you or your precious scheme either."

"There's no harm done, I tell you; none in the least. She has heard nothing."

"How do we know that? Women are so precious artful. If she has been put on by anybody to listen, she has, no doubt, heard more than may be good for us."

"But who could have put her up to listen?"

"How should I know? This Dyot, himself; it is not impossible."

"Why, you silly fellow," replied Anthony, anxious to restore his comrade to confidence and good temper; "when people want to listen without their presence being suspected, they don't usually begin by knocking the furniture about and making a noise?"

"Was that the noise we heard?"

"Nothing else, I assure you. Come into the back kitchen and convince yourself. There is the chair the silly wench stumbled over in the dark, lying on its back, just as it fell. It certainly did seem alarming, but nothing can be more simple than the explanation: her mistress is ill, as I before told you; and, happening to have the key of the back gate with her, she came in that way rather than make a noise by ringing at the front-door bell."

"We'd alter the night if you thought that there was the least danger that she had caught so much as a sentence of our talk," observed Mr. Blake, who, in spite of Mr. Gurd's explanation, was not free from lingering doubt. "One night is as good as another for me."

"Ay, but it isn't for me," replied Mr. Gurd, anxiously and positively; "it must be to-morrow night or not at all. I have very particular reasons for desiring that it should come off to-morrow night. Hang it, man; you don't suppose that I would run the risk if I wasn't sure that all is as safe as can be?"

This last observation of Mr. Anthony seemed to have more weight with the thief than any previous one.

"Very good," said he; "to-morrow night let it be. We need have no further talk about preliminaries? I'll run them over, however, for safety sake. Somebody will pass your shop three times to-morrow —at morning, noon, and evening; and if anything should meanwhile happen to put us off, a yellow wafer will be stuck against the corner bottom pane."

"In the corner right-hand bottom pane," remarked the doctor, precisely.

"And, if all goes well, to-morrow night, at twelve, we shall find the front door easy to open, and a key under the mat that will open *his* door."

"I'll take care."

"The rest you are to leave to us; as far as you can, that is. If he makes a row, you will be very hard to wake; but if you are obliged to put in an appearance, it will be to help us."

"Of course. I help myself when I do so; and you can't have better security than that," replied the candid doctor.

"There will be lots of ways you may help us in the dark, you know. If two men are struggling it's easy to mistake Mr. Right for Mr. Wrong, without a light to see by."

"Exactly; but there's to be no violence —no unnecessary violence."

"'Tain't likely. Why should there be? Where's the advantage to us?"

"None whatever. Another matter there must be no mistake about. *You must take charge of the tin case.* You mustn't let it out of your possession for a single moment after you have once got hold of it. I hope that we understand each other perfectly on that point?"

"I told you so before, didn't I?" said Mr. Blake, impatiently. "I'll look after the case, never fear."

"I shall be on the watch, you understand, although you will not be able to see me; and if all goes right, and you are able to complete the business without any noise being made, you will signal to me as you go down-stairs 'all right' by holding up your hand."

"In this way," observed Mr. Blake, suiting the action to the word.

"And you won't—won't open the case, I was going to say, until we meet the next afternoon at the place agreed on. Of course you'll open it; it isn't in human nature to resist. But you won't take anything out of the case—without putting it back?"

Mr. Blake laughed. "What a suspicious old chap you are! You don't know me as a man of business, or you would never make such an insinuation against my character.

We share together, as we hang together. Well, well; as we stick together, if you like the word better."

And after a few unimportant remarks, Mr. Gurd noiselessly lighted his confederate up to the front door, and let him out, putting the chain on carefully and shooting both the bolts.

"A very clever young fellow," whispered Mr. Gurd to himself, as he stole down to the kitchen again, the muscles of his face relaxing to the expression of an ominous grin; "a nice, affable, plain-spoken gentleman to be sure. Quite a pleasure to deal with him. It's a bold stroke, an awfully bold stroke; but think of the prize! Think of the satisfaction of securing the treasure and avenging one's self on one's enemies at a single sweep!"

And forthwith Mr. Gurd seated himself in a chair by the fire, and proceeded to think, as he had invited himself to do. The operation did not improve the expression of his countenance. Had Mr. Dyot seen it, had he dreamt of it even, as at that moment he lay asleep in his bed, he would have started in affright, mistaking it for one of the ugliest ghosts in his collection broke loose from the iron sepulchre where Doomsday-book was kept.

CHAPTER V.

IS SUGGESTIVE OF THE STORY OF THE MONKEY, THE CAT, AND THE ROASTING CHESTNUTS; WITH A DIFFERENCE AS TO THE LUCK OF THE MONKEY.

"Now, here is a likely story!" says the reader. "This cunning rascal Gurd, this subtle schemer and plotter, despairing of touching the poor gentleman's jealously-guarded treasure, confers and advises with thieves and rogues by profession to attain his ends. Here we have the stoat meeting the fox and politely begging him, since he is so excellent at jumping, to leap over the farmer's fence and procure him [the stoat] a fat pullet or two. Master Blake and the other robber, by Anthony's connivance, are to be admitted into the house, to commit the burglary, to carry off the booty, and fairly and honestly lay it aside till next day, when Mr. Gurd is to come and superintend its equitable division!"

Be not hasty in thy judgment, dear reader. Mr. Anthony Gurd is not the idiot you take him to be, inasmuch as he is ten times a worse one; and, to at once clear away your natural disbelief that such a thing is possible, I will reveal to you the uttermost depths of Mr. Gurd's desperate plan, which was at a single sweep to make him master of the treasure and jewels, and enable him to triumph over his enemies.

It was the doctor's intention to act towards the unlucky thief he had taken into his confidence with deliberate and dastardly treachery. As far as he knew, nobody suspected that he and a ruffian like Blake ever had dealings together. No one had seen the latter enter the house this evening, or was aware of the delicate conference that had taken place between them. As will presently appear, a great deal depended on this, therefore he was, as has already been shown, particularly careful that Mary should not see the "patient" in the kitchen.

To a certain extent, the arrangement made with Mr. Blake was to be executed to the letter. When the burglars came they would discover the way prepared for their easy entry; likewise they would find under the hall-mat a key that would open the door of the intended victim. At this point, however, Mr. Gurd's professed and private designs fell out. According to his contract with Mr. Blake he was to be, as far as circumstances would permit, a sleeping partner in the business; whereas, that he meditated taking an active part in it was sufficiently shown in the fact that within the last day or two an ancient pistol that had long lain idle in a drawer in his bed-room was taken out and well cleaned and oiled ready for service. No ordinary scheme was this secret one of Mr. Anthony, since its security was assured by a double fencing, as it were. In this way. Supposing that, as might possibly happen, the burglars bungled at their work, or they were unable to subdue and silence Mr. Dyot while they plundered his iron safe; supposing that the poor gentleman found in his despair an unexpected amount of strength, and made such an uproar that the house could do no other than be alarmed from top to bottom, then it was Anthony's maturely-considered plan to creep downstairs in the dark, and, under guise of friendship, to approach Mr. Blake and cripple him with a pistol-shot; after which he would be at liberty to assist his outraged lodger in securing the remaining ruffian, and in placing the precious pair in the hands of the authorities. What Mr. Gurd would gain by such a course of procedure was this: he would probably be reinstated in Mr. Dyot's confidence; for how could even so eccentric a gentleman as he was doubt the honesty—nay, the devotedness—of his humble friend after such an exhibition of risk in his behalf? while at the same time he settled the deep grudge he owed against Micah's brother for his insolence and persecution. Although he averred the contrary, he had nourished the hope that the ex-waiter would be the person selected by the more experienced robber to assist him in the burglary, in which case a brace of the birds that were preying on him might be brought down at one cast.

This, if the worst happened and the

burglary failed; provided it was successful a much fuller and fatter harvest would be the result, though poor Master Blake still was doomed to suffer. As already intimated, if the affair came off neatly and quietly, as Blake expressed; if without unnecessary violence (which, of course, did not include the simple tapping of a man on the head with a pistol-butt so as to deprive him of consciousness for a brief space), the chief robber was to make signal of his success by holding up his hand as he passed down the stairs, it being left to the doctor to select a station whence he could descry the said signal. And sure enough, the doctor meant to be on the watch, pistol in hand, and when Master Blake held up his hand, that very instant the barrel of the weapon was to be levelled at the thief's head, Mr. Gurd completing the business by a touch of the trigger.

Nothing, according to Anthony's calculation, could be more certain than that, when the second robber was apprised of the fate of his companion, he would make off with all convenient speed, leaving the field clear for the performance of the crowning act of the plot, which was nothing less than the abstraction from the pocket of the dead or fatally wounded man of the precious jewel-case, to be dealt with as after events dictated. If Mr. Dyot remained insensible, it might even be possible to retain the treasure wholly and entirely, its absence being easily accounted for by the flight of one of the thieves; or, at all events, having possession of it, it was far from improbable that Mr. Dyot might be happy to make just such terms as the doctor chose to name, so that the matter might be hushed up.

"So we go on," his sister Mercy had remarked to him, when first it entered their heads that the best of all ways to keep a man in-doors was to make him too ill to go out—"so we go on, Tony;" and, without doubt, Tony *had* gone on at a rattling pace, indeed, so that now he could even sniff murder and bloodshed not far off without a shudder. There was this to be said, however (and be sure Doctor Gurd did not omit to say it), by the path in life Mr. Blake had of his own free will chosen, his life was forfeited to the law. A burglar caught red-handed was entitled to no mercy; so would say a coroner's jury, so would say his Lordship himself on his judicial bench, if it became a question for him to decide, and, really, the accidental fact of his holding a grudge against the thief had nothing at all to do with it. All such extraneous and trivial circumstance should be dismissed from men's minds when they meet to discuss the solemn question of life and death. "I put it to you, gentlemen of the jury, as fathers of families and peaceful householders, if either of you were startled out of your calm repose in dead of night by an alarm of robbers, would you not do—would you not, at the time and afterwards, feel justified in doing as my client has done?"

Pshaw! If the worst—the very worst of all—came, it was easy enough to foresee how the matter would terminate. And so, bolstered up by the devil within him (if devils have a knowledge of futurity, how the one Anthony was possessed of must have grinned at him!), the doctor, having had his "think" out, took his candle and marched up to bed, and was asleep and snoring; while a much more innocent personage was lying wide awake, filled with vague alarms and puzzling her head as to what use she ought to make of the mysterious conversation she had heard between her master and the ill-looking stranger who appeared so much at his ease.

The individual lying awake was Mary Kettering. From the first she had no doubt that the conversation of Mr. Gurd and the stranger referred to Mr. Dyot, and she was equally convinced that their guilty whispering boded mischief to the poor gentleman. What was the extent of it? What "key" was that they had discussed so anxiously, and what "drawing" that Mr. Gurd had seen made, and for the accuracy of which he could answer? "So I'm to be put off with a miserable third," were the words Mr. Gurd had angrily uttered. And again: "We won't quarrel about our chickens before they are hatched." What was the fair inference to be drawn from this? Why, that the "chickens" were the mysterious riches that Mr. Dyot was supposed to hoard in his strong box, and the drawing was of a key that would open the box. Since the poor gentleman had in so singular a manner informed her of the hard fate in store for "Bertram," although she had seen and spoken to him since several times, he had made no further allusion to the manuscript or any other of his private affairs; but before she slept she resolved that in the morning she would acquaint Mr. Dyot with what she had heard.

It was easy to do this now, for Miss Mercy was confined to her bed and Anthony was not an early riser; whereas Mr. Dyot might be heard stirring in his room soon after daylight. He received her information with considerable amazement, but calmly enough. He was able to corroborate Mary's account in one essential particular—that part of it which related to the drawing of the key. He distinctly recollected the circumstance, even to Mr. Gurd's crumpling up the paper and throwing it out of window.

"It was a piece of ruled paper," said Mary.

"Blue paper, ruled red, like this;" and he took a sheet of similar paper from a drawer. "I remember quite well. So, the prospect of a wretched 'third' did not appear to satisfy this madman! This is not the first time that I have had reasons for holding myself guarded against Mr. Gurd and his sister." And then he told her the story of the poisoned milk—showed her the bottle which he still kept in his cupboard.

"And you never sought to bring them to punishment for it!" exclaimed Mary, indignantly, and none the less so as she thought of the pretty business that the dead-letter drawer had revealed, to say nothing of her own great and deadly spite against Anthony and his sister; "you are content to escape from their clutches, and leave them unhurt and at liberty to practise their monstrous tricks on others! Why are you?"

Mr. Dyot shily avoided the full look that Mary gave him as she asked the sudden question; and she could not but mark his confusion.

"It is surely your duty, sir; especially after this last shameful plot to rob and perhaps murder you."

"Rob me, indeed!" replied the poor gentleman, bitterly; "only that I have nothing to do with revenge, I should be tempted to let them."

"And shall you make no stir in the matter, sir?" asked Mary, anxiously.

"None at all, Mary. It is neither in my disposition nor my interest to do so. I shall go quietly away. This little discovery of yours, my good girl, will not necessitate any alteration in my previous arrangements. I had previously prepared for leaving this place. I shall do so a few hours earlier, that is all. If you will take my advice, you will make your stay with such people as brief as possible. Indeed, I have often wondered——"

"I have a purpose in staying, sir, as you have in going," interrupted Mary.

"It isn't for me, of all men, to pry into the secrets of others," observed Mr. Dyot, smiling sadly as he remarked Mary's sudden embarrassment. "Pardon me if I say this much, however: should you ever need such counsel as an honest man can give or assistance in any way, I trust that you will afford me the opportunity of repaying to the best of my ability a little of the great obligation your goodness has placed me under to you. I am sure that I may trust you. Here is the address where I may be found after to-day. Pray keep it a secret from these people. They will pursue me with their unaccountable persecution if they obtain a clue to my whereabouts, I feel sure."

"What time to-day do you leave, sir?" Mary asked.

"It doesn't matter; any time between this and dark," replied Mr. Dyot; "I shall be pretty sure of frustrating our friend's designs by that means, I suppose. He would scarcely dare break in upon me at daylight?"

"If I were you, sir, I should not leave this house till after dark, if I could avoid it," said the shrewd little woman, after some reflection; "were I in your place, I would not even let them know when I left."

"And why, pray?"

"Because, if they have an interest in knowing where you go, they will follow you."

"To be sure, they will," returned Mr. Dyot, biting his lip in perplexity. "I never thought of that. What, then, shall I do, little counsellor? You have taken my rescue in hand; surely you won't desert me at half way? How am I to get from this abominable place unperceived, Mary?"

"I should delay my going until after dark," replied the little counsellor, after some reflection. "I should delay it until Mr. Gurd went to bed and the house is quiet. I will help you as far as I can."

"I cannot permit that. It is out of the question that you should, for my sake, run a risk of making enemies of these unscrupulous folk. It is merely a matter of withdrawing a bolt and unhooking a chain; and I think that I am clever enough to accomplish that. Thank you, Mary, I will do as you advise. And if I should see you no more between this and then, God bless you, my child! and don't forget that you have my address."

And so he shook hands with her; and no one else in the house was a bit the wiser for their little conversation.

Mr. Anthony was not. He went about his business cheerfully, and nothing that bore the least resemblance to a yellow wafer appeared during the day on any pane of the pill-shop window. Come the evening, however, had anybody observed him closely, it would have been discovered that he betrayed symptoms of nervousness that rapidly increased; and had anybody been curious enough to have applied an eye to the keyhole of the door of the little parlour behind the shop, he would have discovered that more than once or twice Mr. Gurd repaired to a cupboard in the corner where a bottle of brandy found standing room. All went well at present, however, as well and even better than might have been expected. The evening set in dark and gusty, so that the windows rattled and sounds of sudden banging and slamming were not unfrequent. All the better this; if Mr. Blake and his friend should make any noise in opening the street-door or in ascending the stairs, it would the more likely pass unnoticed by anyone lying awake in the house.

What is a bad man's meat is a good man's poison, is a proverb of merit, but it is not true invariably. As on this occasion. The blusterous wind befriended Mr. Gurd's cause, and it likewise served the individual against whom the wicked doctor was digging pits of destruction. Sitting in his own chamber at ten o'clock and past, Mr. Gurd may have heard an unusual noise below, and what sounded amazingly like creaking of stairs and the clinking of a chain, but he recovered his equanimity in an instant. "Pshaw! I am scared by the whining of my own house-dog," said Anthony, grinning to himself, and he pledged the said dog's prosperity in another nip of brandy.

All quiet. Mercy asleep, Mary a-bed, Dyot snug in his cage. Then, in his stockings, Mr. Gurd crept down the stairs to undo the fastenings of the outer door. He discovered them already unfastened. "The careless baggage," growled he to himself, in reference to innocent Mary Kettering. "Is this how she does her duty? This is trusting to servants!" All that remained for Anthony to do was to place a door-key under the mat, and then to steal up-stairs again as noiselessly as he had come down.

It was nearing twelve o'clock now, and

the doctor, deadened in great degree by the brandy he had drank, to the peril of business into which he was presently to plunge, beguiled the time by busying himself with his pistol. Suppose that it should miss fire? It was many a year since it had discharged a bullet. Had he cleaned it properly—loaded it as it should be loaded? Better to be quite sure. And so he set about drawing the charge, and gave the works of the deadly instrument a little more oil, and then reloaded again with great painstaking and precision.

A neighbouring church chimed twelve, and an evil wind, rejoicing that now the play was about to begin, shook the windows as though trying to get in that way, and failing, mounted the roof and squeezed itself with a savage growl down the chimney, occasioning a fall of soot and mortar chips that caused Mr. Gurd to start up with a stifled little cry of terror, pointing his pistol towards the mischief. Then followed a lull, so that the doctor could quite distinctly hear his heart beating, and he would have been glad of a little more brandy, only that he had now extinguished his candle, and was afraid of making a clatter with the bottle and glass.

Then he heard another sound twenty times more startling than the noise in the chimney; a creaking on the stairs below. His door was open, and he crept to it and put his head out. There could be no mistake about it, there was the creak again, and in the tiniest whisper possible he heard a voice say,

"Count ten."

This was the number of stairs to the first flight, as he had instructed Mr. Blake the night before. The burglars were already in the house. So thorough a master of his business was Micah's brother that even a listener had been unable to detect his entrance.

"Now for it!" said Mr. Gurd to himself, screwing up every grain of courage within him. Dropping on to his hands and knees, he crept out on to the landing, peeped between the bannister rails.

"Count ten," whispered the burglar Blake to his companion; and when the ten were counted, "a step and a rise," again whispered Blake, and that brought them on the first landing.

"Now nine." Mr. Gurd, who was all ears, as the saying is, heard plainly enough now; so plain, indeed, that he wondered how the burglars dared speak so loud.

Then he heard quite distinctly the insertion of a key into the lock of Mr. Dyot's door, followed by a muffled exclamation of surprise in the strange man's voice, but the import of which he could not catch.

"They are in the room now; we shall have it in a moment," Anthony repeated to himself, as big drops of sweat trickled down his face. "He will cry out presently; I must be prepared for that."

But nobody cried out. Had not the robbers closed the door he might, however, have heard a whispering that would rather have astonished him.

"Keep him quiet, Mac," Blake said, in a low voice, pointing to the bed dimly visible at the further end of the room.

And Mac, taking a pistol from the breast of his smock, handled it by the barrel clubwise, and stepped up to the bed-side.

"There's nobody here," presently whispered Mac, in hurried tones; "there's nobody slept here to-night. Softly, Teddy, there's something wrong, my boy."

"Not at my end of the room," Teddy whispered back again; "here's the safe, sure enough. That's all we want. He's out, I suppose, and a good job, too, if he doesn't come home in too much of a hurry. D——n this key!"

"Won't it work? Be quick, Teddy! It's a rum go about him being out, though; it's all square, I suppose?"

"B——t my eyes if it is!" exclaimed Blake, as the safe door opened. "It's anything but square, Mac. We're sold! The box is as empty as the bed. I wish I had that shrivelled little whelp here just now, I'd——"

"I knowed there was something amiss," interrupted the other burglar, hastily. "This is a trap, Ted, this is! I'm off! It's only a skip and a jump between this and the street door. Come on! I've got the tools."

All that Mr. Gurd saw, keeping diligent watch through the rails of the bannisters, was first one man and then another emerge precipitately from Mr. Dyot's bed-room.

So far so good; the poor gentleman had been effectually silenced somehow, and the booty was secured without trouble. The first man strode hastily down the stairs; and the other, a taller man, who Anthony knew must be Blake, followed. As the latter was retreating, he ground his teeth savagely, and raising his fist, shook it vengefully at some upper region where the trickster now was. So far so good again; but not, alas! for Mr. Blake. The doctor saw the raised fist, and mistook it for an open hand, whereon he took careful aim, and there followed a tremendous explosion and a cry of pain, and the sound of a helpless man falling headlong down the stairs.

CHAPTER VI.

MARY KETTERING ARRESTS THE ARM OF THE LAW, AND MR. GURD'S BURGLAR-GUEST TAKES WINE WITH HIM.

SCARCELY was the pistol discharged when the cowardly doctor threw it aside, and, taking the stairs three and four at a time, leapt down to where the wounded man lay huddled in a heap. Events seemed to justify Mr. Anthony's calculations in a singularly fortunate manner. He had reckoned, as previously intimated, that when the foremost man heard the discharge of firearms, his movements towards escape would be considerably accelerated. Better even than this happened. Echoing the cry that Teddy Blake uttered, Mac, his companion, sprang towards the street-door, flung it open, and, in his panic lest he should be pursued, slammed it to behind him, so that the assassin had his victim all to himself, and snug as he could desire.

All in the dark, and with desperate dexterity, he hauled Mr. Blake over—for he lay on his face, just as he had fallen—and commenced a scrambling examination of the pockets of the upper part of his dress. As he tore open the front of the jacket that the burglar wore he shuddered as he felt his hand bedabbled, and needed no telling that it was blood. He plunged the wet hand into the breast pocket, where, somehow, he had made sure that he should find the treasure; but, except a great clasp-knife, the pocket was empty.

"D——n! I shall never get on without a light," muttered he; "I would rather have found it before I made any outcry, for fear that *he* should be the first to answer. I wonder——"

But here the little doctor was startled out of his wonderment. Scarcely twenty seconds had elapsed from the time when the pistol was fired. Miss Mercy, lying deep in a feverish sleep, had heard it, and sprang up in her bed in great bewilderment, scarcely knowing whether the noise was real, or part of one of the terribly fantastic dreams that of late had troubled her of nights. The slamming-to of the door, however, convinced her, and jumping out of bed, she seized a constable's rattle that invariably reposed convenient to her hand, and, flinging open the window, began a clatter that might have been heard at the ends of the street.

This unlooked-for proceeding was not at all to Mr. Gurd's taste. Cursing his sick sister for her officiousness, he dropped the senseless man and ran up the stairs nimbly as his legs would carry him, and, without ceremony, dashed into Mercy's room.

"You confounded fool!" cried he; "what are you making that infernal row about?" and, plucking the rattle out of her hand, he shut down the window (which, fortunately, was a back window) with a vehemence that imperilled Mercy's fingers.

"Oh! thank the Lord, you are safe, my dear brother," ejaculated Miss Gurd, whose natural spirit sickness had considerably subdued. "Is it robbers, Tony?—

have they escaped?—are they in the house still? Oh, Lord! there is nothing but trouble lately!"

"There's nothing the matter—at least, not much—not very much. You get into bed. You'll take your death of cold in the state of fever you are in. Give me the lamp, and keep quiet for just a few minutes, and—and I'll bring you up good news, Mercy, dear—the best of news."

The culprit's voice trembled very much as he spoke, though he looked fiercely resolute; and as he laid a persuasive hand on the sleeve of her white night-dress, he left there the imprint of bloody fingers. Sick with fear and terror, she shrank from him, and sank sitting on the bed-side.

"Was *that* what I heard," she said, in an aghast whisper. "Good God, Tony, you never mean to tell me that you have murdered him?"

"Murdered him! murdered who?" asked Anthony, noticing his bloody hand, and making himself look even more like a murderer in his hasty endeavours to wipe it on his shirt sleeve.

"Dyot," replied his sister, in the same

awful whisper. "Is that his blood, Tony?" It is very odd, these vulgar ideas as to the degrees of guilt attaching to the crime of man-slaying.

Mercy, bearing a poor unsuspecting wretch slow poison in his milk-jug could simper and smile with the most innocent face in the world; but she shrank away from her brother's red hand with trembling horror.

Anthony was comforted by his sister's not unnatural mistake. He essayed a little laugh.

"Pshaw! You're making a great fuss about nothing," said he; "Mister Dyot's safe enough—as far as I know, that is. I haven't set eyes on him since this afternoon. Give me the lamp—quick! Don't be afraid. There is no danger; there has been, but it is all over."

"Let me come, too, if there is no danger," returned Miss Gurd, as she planted herself before the lamp, so that her brother might not take it while she hurried on her dressing-gown and slippers. "If there is no danger, there is what I do not understand—what you would conceal from me. More underhand work—more trickery! This is what you call keeping faith with me!"

Considering how she was trembling with excitement, Miss Gurd's dressing occupied marvellously little time, and roused to an assumption of her old airs of command, she took the lamp and led the way, Anthony following.

"Down the stairs," whispered he, grimly, "if you will seek unpleasant sights, why, you must put up with 'em, that's all."

To be sure, it was not the pleasantest of sights that was there to be seen, nor, as it happened, one anticipated to the full by Mr. Gurd himself. Being somewhat unsteady of hand, and labouring under the disadvantage of a bad light, Anthony's aim had not been true, and, instead of speeding a bullet through the burglar's head, as was his deliberate intent, he had but wounded him in the shoulder. The sudden shock, however, and the headlong tumble down the stairs, had effectually reduced Mr. Blake to a condition of insensibility, which probably would have lasted much longer, had it not been for the rough handling to which the doctor had subjected him, in his desperate eagerness to possess himself of the precious jewel-case. As it was, he was just beginning to return to life when Anthony, alarmed by the sound of the rattle, had hurried up to his sister's bed-room; and by the time that the worthy pair were descending together, the robber had so far recovered as to raise himself on one arm; and there he was, pale as death, and with his face horribly smirched, with the clasp-knife Mr. Gurd had felt in the pocket of his jacket, open and clutched with desperate resolution in his right hand. As soon as Mercy saw the ugly spectacle, she uttered a terrified cry, and covered her face with her hands.

"Don't come near me," cried the robber, with a volley of terrible oaths, as he flourished the knife; "don't come within arm's length of me, you white-livered sneak, or I'll cut your throat; I will, by ——! I'll cut your —— head off, if I die and go to hell next minute."

"Who is it?" screamed Mercy. "Tell me who is he? How came he here?"

"He's a burglar, my dear; that's all I know about him. I was aroused by a noise, and I saw him coming out of Mr. Dyot's room and shot him," answered Mr. Anthony, coolly. "You had better go and rouse Mr. Dyot, while I stand here and watch him. Hallo! is that you, Mary? Here's a pretty to-do with robbers in the house! Just fetch me the pistol that I dropped on the next landing, my good girl."

"He's gone! he's gone! he has not slept in his bed to-night."

So cried Mercy, who filled with increased terror and amazement, came from the empty room above, hurrying down the stairs.

"Gone!" was all that Mr. Gurd could ejaculate.

"The safe is open and empty, and he has gone," his sister whispered in his ear.

"Of course the safe is open; this thief forced it," rejoined Anthony, aloud and reckless; "but Dyot *gone*, do you say? Are you quite certain?"

"You knew it well enough, you infernal

villain," spoke Mr. Blake, who, faint through loss of blood, could not regain his feet, though he tried very hard to do so with the assistance of the bannister-rails. "It was a plant from the first. Where's my pal? We'll be square with you yet, you coward—to shoot at a man in the dark! You knew all about this when we talked it over last night."

No wonder that Mr. Gurd was confounded and amazed. As the reader is aware, so far from knowing that Mr. Dyot had fled, he most firmly believed, until his sister had just now revealed to the contrary, that he was a-bed in his room; and now here was his confederate blurting out before Mercy, who he had no doubt, was already moved by certain suspicions, the ugly fact that the night before the robber and himself had held consultation together. Since matters had come to this pass, there was nothing left for it but to show a brazen front.

"What—what is it he says about talking with you last night?" asked Mercy, in a faint voice.

"Tut! What odds what he says?"

returned Anthony, boldly; "who thinks of taking heed of what a detected thief says? Just go to the window—the front window this time—and spring the rattle again. Let us see how many constables' heads this ruffian will cut off when they break in the door."

Mr. Blake, half kneeling, half lying on the mat below, with the dim light of the oil-lamp indistinctly showing his terrible figure, laughed as he heard this.

"I ain't afraid," said he; "spring your rattle and bring 'em in, and let 'em hear my little story. Set about it, quick!"

"Too quick for you, you ruffian!" exclaimed Mr. Gurd; and with that he stepped past his sister to hasten to the front room; but there, in his path, stood Mary Kettering.

"You had better not bring the constables here," she whispered, so that no one else heard.

"And why not? What have you to do with it. Pray, are you one of the gang?" exclaimed Anthony, furiously.

"Hush! It was to be a gang of three only, if you recollect," replied Mary, knowing what she knew, and courageous in her knowledge. "Three only, and you were to have but a wretched third of the plunder."

Mr. Gurd no longer endeavoured to pass on to the front room that he might spring his rattle out o' window; he was glad to lay his hand on the stair-rail to steady himself.

"What do you mean?" he inquired, in a shaky voice, and feebly attempting to make bluster pass for virtuous indignation. "Dare you accuse me of——"

"Of obtaining a drawing of the key of Mr. Dyot's strong-box, that you might use it or cause it to be used to-night? Yes, I dare accuse you of that. I dare accuse you of more, and I will, if you persist in turning traitor on this poor wretch."

Bluster was of no use in the face of a witness such as this, and before he could make up his mind what answer to make, there came a knocking at the street-door.

"There are the constables; let them in," exclaimed Mr. Blake himself.

But Anthony did nothing of the kind.

"My dear," said he, hurriedly, whispering to his sister, "they must not come in. There is some terrible mistake here which I will explain to you by and by. The constables must not see this ruffian; we must hide him."

"Where can we hide him?" replied Mercy, in a hard, dry voice. She had no doubt, by this time, that her brother had blundered into a more formidable nest of hornets than ever. "How can we go near him, after his threats?"

"You may come near me safely enough. Since I've drawn your teeth, you needn't fear mine," observed the burglar, coolly; and with a jerk, he tossed the knife up to Mr. Gurd. "There's no occasion to hide me; say that I'm a lodger here, and that you shot me by mistake."

"And you'll keep your tongue still?" remarked Mr. Gurd, in a low voice, as he descended the stairs.

"As long as you make it worth my while, I will."

Whereon Mr. Gurd stept to the door and opened it, and in walked two constables.

"Beg your pardon, sir, but was it here

that——Ay, it's all right, I see," continued he, flashing the strong light of his lantern into the passage. "It's all right, Bill; out with the bracelets."

"It was here that the rattle was sounded," replied Mr. Gurd, in his most affable tones—"most foolishly sounded, as it turns out. It's all a mistake, gentlemen—a most unfortunate mistake for this young man, who is a lodger of mine, you must know. Go to bed, Mercy, my dear. I'll see after poor Mr. Tomkins. He isn't much hurt—merely a flesh wound. You see, gentlemen [this in a low voice, so that the delicate ear of Tomkins might not suffer offence], this foolish young fellow will drink; and when he drinks he's as nigh mad as can be—goes about the house of nights and plays all manner of pranks. He did so to-night; and I thought, to be sure, that there were burglars in the place, and seeing him creeping down the stairs, I fired at him, and unluckily grazed him on the shoulder. It isn't much. I'm a doctor, and I know, of course."

"Lucky it ain't no wuss, for you as well as him, sir. Let's have a look at him," observed Bill; and he approached the prostrate burglar with his lantern. But Mr. Blake had his cue, and most persistently lay with his arm across his face, so that even his most intimate friends, the constables, failed to recognize him.

"I suppose that you'll be getting him to bed again," remarked one of the men. The circumstance of Mr. Blake having, after the fashion of expert burglars, kicked off his boots as soon as he entered the house, favoured the supposition of his being a lodger in the house.

"He'll have to be got to bed again; oh, yes, exactly so!" replied Mr. Gurd, though not without considerable hesitation.

"We may as well give you a lift up with him, sir, now we are here; he's none of the lightest, judging from his build; and he's a long way from sober yet, as anybody may see. Bear a hand, Bill, while the gentleman goes first with the light and shows us the room."

The women—Miss Mercy and Mary Kettering, that is—had by this time disappeared; and Mr. Gurd, with all apparent civility, though in reality grinding his teeth with fury, went forward with the lamp, the two constables following, and handling their burden with praiseworthy tenderness. Mr. Dyot's room-door still stood open, and in at it the doctor turned.

"This is his room," said he. "Dear, dear! he hasn't been to bed at all! That will do, constables; lay him down. I can manage him now; and here's half a guinea for your trouble."

Just at this moment one of the men caught sight of the door of the safe in the wall swung wide open.

"Hallo! blest if he ain't been committing of a burglary on himself!" said he.

"Oh! that's nothing—merely an old box left here by a previous lodger; it is seldom or never locked," Mr. Gurd hastened to remark. "That will do, thank you; I won't trouble you to stay any longer." It wasn't so much on account of Mr. Blake that he was anxious for the departure of the constables as because of Mary Kettering. Ever since she had whispered those astounding words to him, he had laboured under a vague terror that matters were worse even than they appeared. "There is much more that I know and dare tell," she had said. What security had he against her altering her mind and coming down to relate to the officers all that she knew?

"If he should break out again, you know, sir, me and my mate won't be far out of earshot," remarked one of the constables, in a whisper, as the doctor showed them down the stairs.

"Oh! you need not trouble;" but then, as though suddenly bethinking, "I mean to say that I shall not trouble you unless I am downright obliged [this he said quite loud enough for Mr. Blake to hear]; if I should need your assistance, you will be within earshot, as you say. Good-night!"

And with that he shut the door and secured it. There was a little red pool at the stairs' foot, and as he hurried forward, Mr. Gurd put one stockinged foot in it, staining every stair as he ascended, a fact which he did not discover until he reached the top of the flight, his temper being by no means improved by the discovery. As he was about to re-enter the room lately occupied by Mr. Dyot, the door of Mercy's chamber opened, and she called to him to come in. He saw that Mary Kettering was with his sister.

"I will be with you presently. I've a little business to settle here first," he replied; and in order that Mercy might quite understand that the business he alluded to must not be interrupted, when he entered the room where the wounded man was lying, he locked the door on the inside. It seemed that his carriage up the stairs had rather a refreshing influence than otherwise on Mr. Blake, for he was half reclining, half sitting on Mr. Dyot's bed, and was holding his handkerchief to his hurt shoulder.

"Be quick; come and stop this infernal bleeding," exclaimed the burglar, impatiently. "I'm growing as weak as a cat."

"Before we go any further," Mr. Gurd exclaimed, affecting tremendous determination, perhaps you'll be good enough to explain what this—this dodge about the empty chest means? You had better. I am not a man to be trifled with. I have convinced you of *that*, I presume?"

"Before we go any further, give me something to drink," growled Mr. Blake. "What's in that bottle? it's brandy, isn't it?"

"You insolent scoundrel?" exclaimed Mr. Gurd, handling the bottle (it was sherry, not brandy) by the neck, as though of a good mind to launch it at the crippled man's head. What is to hinder my poisoning you, stabbing you, beating your brains out, like a dangerous whelp, as you are? Do you think I haven't the will to do it?"

"I'm sure that you've the will, and that you'd do it but for one thing," replied Teddy. His assurance had not all leaked out at the hole in his shoulder.

"For what one thing, pray? Because of what?"

"Because I've a friend in court. Because there have been eyes on you when you haven't in the least suspected 'em," replied Blake, grinning. "But there, give us the bottle, man; my tongue is like a dried fish-skin."

And, fairly staggered by this answer, Mr. Gurd mechanically handed the wounded thief the bottle, who uncorked it with his teeth, and, after a satisfactory sniff at its contents, took a long drink.

"That's better," said he, as he set the bottle down. "If I'm no worse than I feel there's not much the matter, after all. You had better go and fetch some plaster and bandage, hadn't you? Look alive!"

In the heat of his indignation, Mr. Gurd was about to reply that he would see the burglar in the most undesirable place within or without the world ere he would attend to his injury; but it instantly occurred to him that if he wished, as he most sincerely did, to see the back of his decidedly unwelcome guest, he could not do better than help him to a fit condition for taking his departure. Besides, although Mr. Blake seemed to have rallied considerably from the shock, it was far from impossible that his pistol wound might not, after all, be attended with fatal results; and it would be worse than all to have the thief dead on his hands. Mr. Blake noticed his hesitation.

"Don't be afraid that I shall hurt you if you come nigh me," he observed, with an expression of contempt. "I ain't your match just now. You knocked me over, you —— coward, you! and you must set me up again; then we'll see about squaring our reckoning."

"I am not afraid of you, why should I be?" returned Mr. Gurd. "It was all a mistake, my shooting you, I tell you. I could not see well, it was so dark; and—and I mistook you for Dyot himself following in pursuit of you. There! now you know the hinge on which the whole misfortune turns."

Mr. Blake listened to this simple statement with unfeigned incredulity, and looked as though he was about to express it in unmistakable terms; but he turned his wrath to a grin, and shook his head.

"Get out the plastering," said he. "I don't want to hear anything you have to say until you have done that."

"You must tell me one thing before I move a hand to help you; and I tell you plainly that you'll bleed to death in an hour if I don't help you?"

"*Must* tell you! What must I tell you?"

"What you meant when you said that you had 'a friend in court?' Who's your friend? I think I can guess pretty close to the mark; but I want to hear it from your lips. Whose eyes 'have been on me when I haven't suspected it?'"

"Whose! why, the girl's. Guess, indeed! I should rather think it was past guessing after what she whispered to you atop of the stairs. I heard what she said; every word."

"So, so! Hers were the eyes that watched me when I least suspected it! I see it all now. She is a woman of your gang, and this has been an arranged business from the first."

"No; by ——, you're wrong!" cried out Blake, starting up with such energy that his wound began again to bleed apace. "If what you know of her don't convince you that it can't be, take my word for it that you never were more wrong in all your life. She our sort! She looks it, don't she? No. She was so kind—Lord knows why—to save me from the traps; and I won't have her dragged into this infernal mess. I'd sooner bleed to death; I would, by ——"

And the wretched thief, with the fading fire of manliness within him for an instant fanned into a flame, spoke with tears in his eyes.

"D'ye mean to tell me that you never spoke with her—never saw her before to-night?" exclaimed Anthony, already half convinced by the robber's manner that his suspicions were unfounded.

"I mean to tell you that I never spoke to her, and that I never saw her before I looked through the chink of the kitchen door and saw her speaking with you last night," answered Mr. Blake, truthfully. "You talk like a fool, man. What she whispered to you was part of our talk last night. Have I since then had a chance of speaking with her?"

To be sure he had not. To Mr. Gurd's knowledge, Mary had not left the house for a moment throughout the preceding day.

"The devil's in it, I believe," said he, passing his hand across his forehead in a bewildered way; and without another word he took the lamp and went in search of dressing for the burglar's hurt.

CHAPTER VII.

MR. GURD AND HIS GUEST ENGAGE IN THE PLEASANT GAME OF "DOG BITE DOG."

As already intimated, Mr. Blake was not dangerously hurt. The treacherous bullet that Mr. Gurd had aimed at him, missing its mark, had struck the burglar on the round of his shoulder, and, after ploughing along the surface for two inches or more, passed out at his coat collar and flattened against the wainscot. An ugly scratch to look at, and one from which enough blood had flowed to saturate completely the upper portion of the burglar's garments, and reduce him to the verge of fainting; but this was the extent of the damage. Careful treatment and a fortnight's rest would set the limb in as sound and serviceable a condition as ever.

But the doctor, after an examination

of the injury, thought fit to make out to his patient that the accident was of an even more trivial character than it was. It was to his interest to do so. There was nothing to be gained by detaining Mr. Blake on the premises. On the contrary, he was altogether an objectionable and unprofitable guest, and the sooner he took his departure the better.

"What's the damage?" Mr. Blake inquired, when the doctor had completed his survey. "Any bones broke?"

"Not so much as grazed: a mere cat's scratch," replied Anthony, as he busied himself over the wound. "You may congratulate yourself on your good luck, my friend."

"I may, and I may not; that's my affair. You attend to yours," growled the sick thief, wincing at the bandaging.

"It was a very fortunate circumstance," continued Mr. Gurd, not heeding the interruption, "an extremely fortunate circumstance, that, mistaking you for that scoundrel Dyot, and being so anxious lest he should overtake you, my aim was dis-

"I know all about it. Who's grumbling about the luck? I shan't grumble till I find occasion to; and it won't be my fault if I *do* find occasion, take my word for it," the burglar answered, meaningly.

"Just what I say, my friend; you should *not* grumble. If you knew the precious close shave you have had, you wouldn't think of doing so. No; it is I that have cause for grumbling. It's bad enough for you, but worse for me—twenty times worse."

"I'm glad that you have made up your mind to it," returned the robber, grimly; "it's half the battle when you've made up your mind."

"What do you mean?"

"Why, that this little business will cost you something more than a trifle. I never do a job for nothing. I've engaged at this, and very well I know it [this with a rueful glance at his shoulder], and it has got to pay me."

"Pay you?"

"Ah! by —— it has. D'ye mean to say that you didn't know it? You'll know me better before we shake hands."

And Mr. Blake nodded his head with a determination that chilled Mr. Anthony's blood to contemplate. From the time when, acting on the mysterious hint furnished him by Mary Kettering, he had misled and dismissed the constables, repudiating the burglary and acknowledging Mr. Blake as, if not a peaceful, at least a respectable lodger, the dread that the latter would take advantage of it had haunted him.

"How?" he asked, pretending to misconstrue the robber's hint. "Perhaps you know where Dyot has fled to. Do you?—do you, young man? I'd give twenty pounds to hear you say 'yes.' *Do* you know where he has gone?"

"I don't know, and I don't care; it's no business of mine. I don't want to dip into the lucky bag with both hands. You may look after him and make the most of him when you find him. *I mean looking after you.* Make no mistake."

There could be no mistake. Half the light that the dim lamp gave would have been sufficient to have read the firmly-settled purpose visible in Mr. Blake's countenance.

"Now, this is what I call gratitude! This is returning good for good, this is!" exclaimed the doctor, with a prodigious effort to speak with severe sarcasm. "I rescue you from the grasp of the law; I have you carried to my bed; I give you wine; I bind up your wounds; and now——"

"You've looked after me, and now I mean to look after you," interrupted the burglar, with a laugh. "You won't be able to reckon it up better than that, if you preach for a month. Bah! you thundering old leech! You confounded old Jeremy Diddler! D'ye think I haven't found you out? And d'ye imagine that I'll spare you? We shall see."

"You've drank too much wine. Your blood is inflamed. You'll be less violent in your language when you call on me to-morrow." And, though the doctor tried to speak with calmness, his voice absolutely trembled with fury. "How far is it from this to your lodging?"

"No distance at all. I'm lodging here for the present."

"Quite so. But you are naturally

anxious to get home to—to your friends. They will be on thorns as to what has become of you. You feel pretty well now that your arm is bound up, don't you?"

"Pretty well, thanky. Let us have a bit of fire, and I'll finish the sherry over a pipe," replied the burglar, grinning at the rage and consternation visible in the little doctor's face. "Don't trouble yourself about my friends, old gentleman. I'll get you to run down to Spitalfields in the morning to tell them how I am getting on. Don't let me disturb your domestic felicity. Just fetch up some wood and coals, and you can go to bed as soon as you like."

This was too much.

"Look you here, you scoundrel!" exclaimed Mr. Gurd, shaking his little fist at the robber with the courage of despair. "You think you've got the upper hand of me in this business!"

Mr. Blake, who was now sitting up on the bed, and had contrived to fill his pipe and light it, blew out a cloud of smoke, and nodded by way of affirmative.

"There you are mistaken. You heard

that the constables promised to keep within call?"

Another nod.

"Suppose I call them. Suppose I have them here and swear that I was mistaken when I thought that you were merely an innocent, tipsy man wandering about my house in the night, and that in reality you are a designing thief, who—who, first of all," continued Mr. Gurd, the fertility of his imagination increasing with his warmth —"who, first of all, and aided by my woman-servant, decoy out of my house a gentleman of wealth who is staying here, that you two may rob him with impunity, she assisting you into the house."

"That I have robbed the old safe—the safe left here by a former lodger, gentlemen," remarked Mr. Blake, pleasantly imitating the tone as well as the words that the doctor had used when addressing the constables on the subject.

"That you and this woman have planned and executed this precious plan between you," continued Mr. Gurd, not heeding the interruption. "Do you see, shallow-brains? Do you see, you insolent, swaggering rascal? It is I who have the upper hand—the hand that will put a rope round your neck. Now, what do you say?"

"I say that it's precious cold without a fire, and that if you don't step down and see about one I shall be obliged to touch the bell here and summon the woman you just alluded to to do so for me. I'll ring the bell, anyhow, so that the woman—the woman, you know, who put up this robbery with me—may hear what you've got to say about her. I can't bear to hear people talked about behind their backs."

And thereon, although Mr. Gurd hastily stepped forward to prevent the act, the burglar put up his hand to the bell-pull that hung at the bed-head, and rang a peal that might have been heard from basement to garret.

CHAPTER VIII.

IN WHICH MARY KETTERING, BY AN UNGUARDED SLIP OF THE TONGUE, GIVES HER ENEMIES A FRESH START FOR THE WINNING-POST.

Affrighted by the dismal apprehension that the clamorous ringing at the bell in the lodger's bed-room portended at least the attempted strangulation of her brother Anthony, Miss Mercy Gurd, albeit attired merely in her morning wrapper and with her wan, lay-a-bed face set round with the frills of her unhandsome night-cap, rushed swiftly to the rescue. Her terrors had restored to her for the time the strength that naturally belonged to her, but which had been sadly relaxed by fever; and easily, as though she were a child, as she hurried from one room to the other, she hauled along with her, holding her wrist with a tight grip, Mary Kettering.

From the fact of Mary being hauled along, it may be inferred that she came unwillingly. She did so. She could not but feel that matters had assumed a complexion much more sombre than she had anticipated when she volunteered her good services towards setting wrong right.

Not even Mercy herself was more astonished than Mary when she heard the pistol-shot, and her great fear was either that Mr. Dyot had altered his mind about taking a secret departure (for, though she was more than half-convinced that she heard the door-chain clink as the poor gentleman put it from its fastening, she was not positive of the fact) or that for some purpose he had returned, and that there had been a murderous encounter between him and Mr. Anthony. Great, indeed, was her amazement when, hastily slipping a cloak over her night-dress, she emerged from her garret and descended the stairs, candle in hand, to discover her master half dressed, and all blood-bespattered, his sister clinging to him in bewildered terror, and the flashy young fellow whom she had seen puffing at his cigar as he examined Mr.

Gurd's curious "drawing" couched on the mat below, stained as Anthony was, and with a great clasp-knife open in his hand. If it had transpired that the poor gentleman had shot the robber in self-defence, Mary, who had been witness to that worthy's cool manner of planning the atrocity, would have felt but little pity for him; but when she heard Mr. Gurd acknowledge to the shooting, justifying it by a cowardly and audacious falsehood, it seemed to her that, since one villain must go to the wall, that should be the fate of the most inveterate, and her consequent course of action together with its result, the reader has already been made acquainted with.

"I am glad that you are come!" exclaimed Mr. Anthony, as his sister appeared. "We can do without *you*," continued he, looking furiously at Mary, who came after her mistress, and catching the edge of the door, the doctor made as though to slam it in the face of his mischievous maid-of-all-work.

"You had better let her in," exclaimed Mercy. Expecting to discover her brother in the agonies of death, when she found him looking as well, nay, if anything, more vigorous than when she last saw him, her solicitude in his behalf turned straight to spite. "You may shut her out, but you can't shut out what she knows. This fellow here still? How long is he to stay, pray?"

Mr. Blake's shoulders were bare, for the convenience of his surgical dressing; but on the entry of the ladies, he modestly pulled the counterpane about them.

"It quite depends on circumstances, my dear madam, how long this fellow is going to stay," said the robber, bowing politely to Miss Gurd. "You may depend on it, however, that he won't stay an hour longer than suits him. Your brother and myself are partners, you see, old lady; and it isn't easy to turn away a partner at a minute's notice."

Miss Gurd turned from the occupant of the bed in ineffable disgust. "Why did you ring?" she asked of her brother.

"He did not ring, ma'am; it was me," replied Mr. Blake, with a greater show of politeness than ever, observing that the "old lady" did not like it. "I rang, ma'am, because your brother, my respected partner, had begun to say something damaging to the character of the young person here, and I thought it better that she should be present to hear it."

"I have no desire to be present. I have no wish to mix further in this dreadful affair. I regret that I have interfered so far," exclaimed Mary, much agitated. "I had much rather leave the house now, this instant. It is no place for an honest woman." And she turned to the door, against which Miss Gurd set herself, however.

"And when will you go, Madame Honesty?" said Mercy, sneeringly. "Surely you had better stay till the morning. Your excellent friend, Mr. Dyot, is ailing, remember, and is not likely to be sitting up for you till this hour."

Fires of indignation quenched the tears in Mary's eyes instantly as she heard these words.

"Don't taunt me!" she exclaimed, facing round at Miss Mercy in a way that made even that resolute lady back a step; "don't make me a more bitter enemy towards you than I now am. If you drive me to open my mouth to its fullest against you, I will, if you and your brother hang for it!"

"Hear, hear!" remarked Mr. Blake, with an approving grin. "I say, old lady, what about hanging, eh? S'help if I don't begin to feel like a innocent young feller beguiled into bad company. But you're a-joking, young woman; you couldn't really hang 'em now, could you? What could you hang 'em for? Don't mind letting it out before me; I'm a partner, you know."

But neither Anthony nor his sister heard a word of Mr. Blake's jocular remarks; their minds were too fully occupied by the strange threat their servant had so earnestly uttered.

"Our bitter enemy, are you? How comes that?" inquired Mercy, affecting a sneer of cool indifference, but in reality hotly anxious to know what the words implied. "Pray, what kitchen troubles have we imposed on you that make you our bitter enemy."

"Don't ask. I have said too much, as it is," replied Mary (and she really thought so). "Let me go."

"It's all very fine to say 'let you go,'

young woman," remarked Mr. Blake, whose hurt was at ease, and who by this time had drank enough of the sherry to restore his natural flow of humour. "You tell that to the Lord Mayor when you're took before him. We can't let such characters as you go at large—no, not even on bail; can we, partner?"

And as he concluded, the robber favoured Mary with a confidential wink, intended to convey "Only a bit of a game. Don't mind me. You'll learn what I'm driving at in a minute if you will give attention." But Mary could not at all see the fun of it.

"I don't know what you are talking of. I would rather that you did not speak to me," said she, turning from Mr. Blake.

"And you think to get off like that, do you?" persisted the robber, in high good-humour, and thinking, possibly, that the young woman had turned away to conceal her recognition of the joke. "P'r'aps you'll alter your tune when you hear what my partner here intends to do with you. A wide-awake old person my partner is, my dear; and it is no use your trying to get over him. He has found out all about you. It was you, you know, who planned this robbery with me and my friends; it was you who beguiled away the gentleman that used to occupy this apartment in order that the crack might come off all the easier; it was you who came down to-night and let us in. There's no use in your denying it, young woman. As true as I'm a living man, my partner here swore hard and fast not ten minutes ago that that was the charge he meant to bring against you. The constables are still within hail, and he intends to call them presently and repeat to them all that I've just told you. Ain't I speaking what's true, partner?"

"I wish to the Lord that I had sent a bullet through your ugly head," exclaimed Mr. Gurd, snarling like an angry dog. "If you were got rid of, you scoundrel, the way would be easy enough."

"I'm sure that I don't want to be in anybody's way," returned the burglar, laughing. "You'll excuse my putting my spoke in, partner. I saw that you didn't have pluck enough to tell her yourself, else I shouldn't."

"Is it true?" asked Mary Kettering, turning to Mr. Gurd. "Is it true, as this man says, that you dared to think of fastening this robbery upon me? I wish that you would do so. I would rather you did that than anything."

"Why would you?" Mercy asked.

"Because it would be the shortest way for me out of this trouble—the shortest way and the easiest, as it seems," Mary replied.

"What! so that you might raise your virtuous voice against us and free yourself at our cost? No doubt you would be listened to with all the respect you are deserving of! He! he! An unfortunate young woman who was thankful to pay down money security to obtain a place as kitchenmaid rather than send her employer for the character that she knew was her due!"

Once again Mary's eyes flashed dangerously, but she controlled her anger.

"You do not, or will not understand me," said she. "I should send for Mr. Dyot; he would stand my friend."

"You would send for Mr. Dyot, eh?"

spoke Anthony, directing a swift look full of eager meaning at his sister. "Would you be content to lie in prison until your messenger found him?"

"Pshaw! She has his address, no fear of that," answered Miss Gurd; "didn't she just now say as much?"

"Yes, I have his address," replied Mary, her prudence yielding before her momentary impulse to triumph over her enemy; "I have but to hand his address to the first person I meet, and Mr. Dyot may be found in half an hour."

But Mr. Gurd looked not at all like a man overwhelmed and crushed by this item of intelligence. On the contrary, he licked his lips as though Mary's observation had imparted to the air a flavour that was to his taste. Once more he glanced at Mercy, who responded by another glance, and, as it happened, neither one glance nor the other was lost on Mr. Blake, although he seemed thoroughly engaged with the sherry-bottle.

"It is of much more importance to you than to us that you know where Mr. Dyot is," remarked Mercy, with a sneer, that gave full meaning to her words. "You have managed him very cleverly, no doubt."

"Once more I tell you——"

"No, don't, if you take my advice, young woman," put in the friendly burglar. "You've told too much already, if I'm not mistaken. You ain't used to deal with such a pair of foxes as these are, my girl. Take a friend's advice, and shut your mouth, and keep it shut till you are fairly out of this den."

"I'm sure I shall be heartily glad to see both you and her out of it," remarked Mr. Gurd. "But she mustn't leave till morning. I don't want any further attention drawn to my house in one night, I can assure you. Matters must remain as they are till to-morrow, I suppose." And the doctor affected to look mightily dissatisfied that he was compelled to assent to any such arrangement.

"I would rather go at once. I don't feel safe staying here," said Mary.

"Is there a lock to your door, young woman?" inquired Mr. Blake.

"Pshaw! what rubbish!" exclaimed

Anthony. "Who wants to hurt *you*, do you think? We want to arrange matters quiet and comfortable, and not to break out afresh. There is the room in front of my sister's chamber that overlooks the street: stay there till the morning, if you are afraid to sleep in your back attic."

"Which floor is that on?" inquired Mr. Blake.

"On this floor?"

"And where do *you* sleep, partner?"

"Partner be hanged! On the floor above is where I sleep."

"That will do, then. Take my advice, young woman, and finish the night in the front room they speak of. You are all right. *I shan't go to sleep.*"

"The fire is laid, and there is a sofa in the room, so your ladyship won't come to much harm," remarked Miss Gurd, with a titter.

"I will do as you ask," replied Mary, after a little consideration, feeling a confidence in Master Blake that was not a little strange, seeing that by this time she was aware that he was a robber by profession.

As Mercy and her maid-servant turned out of the consultation-chamber the church chimes were striking two.

"You are going to bed, too, I presume?" remarked Mr. Gurd to the burglar, and in a much more gracious tone than he had hitherto adopted; "there is no use in sitting up all night."

"I was thinking that we might have a bit of fire and another bottle of sherry; it seems a pity to break up so early, now that we are such good friends," rejoined Mr. Blake, in his most free-and-easy manner. "What do you say?"

"I'd rather be excused, thankye. There's a good deal to be thought of between this and the morning. I must go to bed, though I don't suppose that I shall sleep much," replied the doctor, becoming fidgety, and looking as though he much wanted to get away, though afraid to betray his desire.

Blake laughed, as he regarded Mr. Anthony, in a queer kind of way.

"No," said he, "I don't expect that you will sleep much."

"And why not, pray?"

"Why not!" and the queer expression vanished as if by compulsion; "why, for fear that I should be coming up in the dark to cut your throat. You have given me provocation enough, haven't you?" However, the burglar still spoke in a jocular way.

"Thankye; I'm not in the least afraid of that. I've got a good lock and bolt to my door, and I shall take precious good care to use them."

"Ah! because you ain't the least afraid. Is there a bolt to *my* door?"

"Strong enough for a bank. He was infernally fond of bolts and bars; curse him! There'll be no fear of anyone breakin on *you*, Mr. Blake."

"They won't have occasion to. If they want me they can get at me without trouble. I shall get a snooze with the door open."

"Please yourself," responded the doctor, shrugging his shoulders. "Shall I leave you the lamp."

"No, thankye; there's moonlight enough for me; be off."

And Mr. Gurd went off, taking the lamp with him.

"I'd better pull the door to a little, hadn't I?" said he, as he was going out, and suiting the action to the word, "there, that much!"

"Put it back; put it wide open, I tell you," replied Mr. Blake, with the obstinacy and thick utterance of a half-tipsy man, "that's better."

"It doesn't matter; he'll be snoring asleep in ten minutes," said Mr. Gurd to himself, as he made his way up to his bedroom.

"There's a new game afloat, unless I'm much mistaken," muttered Blake, suddenly looking perfectly sober. "I'm with you, partner. You get a rise out of me, and I'll forgive you."

Then Mr. Blake got off the bed, and made bustle enough for Mr. Gurd to hear, as though he were preparing to make himself comfortable for the remainder of the night. Then he lay down, and, after a reasonable time, took to snoring, gently at first, and more vehemently by degrees—with his eyes open.

He might so have passed a quarter of an hour, when—still snoring—he raised his head from the pillow a little, and inclined his ear to the open door. There was not much to hear: a mouse running up a wainscot makes a noise ten times as loud, but it was enough for Mr. Blake. It is not often that a man snores with such a grin of intelligence as that which overspread the burglar's face at that moment.

Mr. Gurd was out of his bed-room and at the stair-head listening. Having cautiously descended two stairs, he sat down with his hand behind his ear, and so remained for ten minutes at least, still as a wooden image.

But Mr. Blake, made aware that now was the time for an exhibition of his skill, enacted the half-drunken sleeper to a miracle. He snored now with his mouth open and a-dry, and this was a harsh, loud-sounding snore; then his parched mouth disturbed him, and he closed it with a feeble clucking sound, as though in his sleep he was endeavouring to moisten his dry lips with his drier tongue. Then for a brief space he snored the muffled snore of a man who has his mouth closed; and as the mouth fell helplessly ajar, gradually, so, gradually, did the snore increase in volume.

All these various symptoms of heavy sleeping were noted by the experienced doctor with immense satisfaction.

"A pretty fellow to be on guard!" was Anthony's mental ejaculation, as he rose from his lonely seat. "Like all these low, bragging ruffians, they can talk, and that's all."

The low, bragging ruffian in question rose in bed—snoring the while—at exactly the same moment as the doctor rose from the stair; and sliding off his couch noiseless as a shadow, he approached the door.

He heard that Mr. Gurd was in his room.

He heard that Mr. Gurd was coming out of his room, whereon he glided back to the bed, and, bending over it, snored melodiously; at the same time, without the least noise, feeling for his jacket, that lay on the bed, and for the pocket of it, to which he had long since restored his knife. By the time he had transferred the weapon from one pocket to another, he heard that

Mr Gurd was on the move again—this time in an upward direction; so he ventured, after waiting a little, to rise and creep out of the room to the landing.

Up the stairs stole Anthony, with a candle in one hand and in the other no more formidable implement than a screw-driver, bound for Mary Kettering's bedroom.

CHAPTER IX.

TREATS OF STRANGE DISCOVERIES.—THE ELDER "PARTNER" PROVES HIMSELF THE KEENEST OF THE TWO.—MR. GURD GIVES HIS MIND TO PRISON ARRANGEMENTS.

ALTHOUGH Mr. Gurd was by this time pretty well assured that he had nothing to fear from the exhausted and tipsy man snoring on the bed below, it was necessary that he should move with caution, for doubtless Mary was awake, and it would not do for her to hear. A-tiptoe, therefore, and stepping very softly indeed, he strode up the stairs leading to the back attic; and there he proceeded to his task with celerity. Behind the door hung the gown which Mary had worn on the previous day, and into the pocket of it the doctor plunged his sacrilegious hand without scruple; but he found nothing that in the least concerned him except the key of the box. This was something, however.

Placing the candle on the floor, he was down on his knees and at the box in an instant. His search was not immediately rewarded, however, and it was not until he had taken out fully one-half of the contents of the box that he made any discovery worth speaking of. Then he made one of a sort that he had not bargained for, and it amazed him rather. This was the letter that Mary had purloined from the drawer—the letter that Mrs. Craven had sent containing the intelligence of "little Osborne's" death, together with the precious little lock of curly black hair.

"What on earth does *this* mean!" exclaimed Anthony, under his breath. He knew the letter at once. He had reason to remember it. It was the herald of a piece of good luck such as falls to a man's share but rarely. "How came she by this? However, this is no time to think about it." And so saying, he thrust the letter containing the precious little curl into his trousers-pocket, and continued his overhauling.

His next find was of much more satisfactory character—it was an address. There was no name; but he had no doubt as to whose hands it had passed through, for the writing was on the identical blue paper ruled red, such as Mr. Dyot was so constantly in the habit of using. "17, Rufford's Terrace, close by Stangate, Westminster."

"It is a long lane that has no turning," whispered the doctor, with a joyful sigh; "the luck seemed dead set against me; but here's a slice at last, a fat slice, we'll have no vagabond fingers in the pie this time." And the address was thrust into the pocket to keep company with Mrs. Craven's letter.

"Is there anything else, I wonder?" thought he; he could afford to dally a little now that he had secured his prize. There were a few other scraps of loose papers and a few old letters of her old lover, baby's father, but they were not addressed to the old harness-maker's house, but to the residence of a friendly old lady in an adjoining street, with which, as well as the old lady's name, Anthony was quite unfamiliar. Presently, however, he picked up a partly-torn letter cover. The upper half was torn away, but the full address remained: "The Harness-maker's, close to the Palace Gates, Kensington."

Had there been a wasp in the paper, Mr. Gurd could not have given a more sudden start as he read the superscription by the candlelight. A sound of some kind was emitted from his lips, but only that it was expressive of extreme amazement, was otherwise unintelligible.

At that instant, however, a hand was thrust over his shoulder, and the paper plucked from his grasp.

"Halves, partner!"

The reader need not be told who it was that cried halves, or of the speechless terror that seized on the little doctor as the words were uttered. Mr. Blake's was the grinning face that met his own as with a start of horror he turned his head; with mock politeness the robber bowed as he pocketed the address.

"You've read it, so it can't be of any further use to you," said Mr. Blake. "I might want, one of these fine days, to make a call myself on the gentleman that this relates to."

Taken all aback by the suddenness of the attack and eager only for a return fling at his assailant, Mr. Gurd nearly did a rash thing.

"Yes, you scoundrel!" said he, in as low a voice as Blake had spoken, "I have read it, and you may read it; now what do you suppose it to be?"

"I couldn't guess if I was to try for a month," replied Blake, affecting an expression of innocence. "It isn't the bit of writing that your gal got of Dyot, I suppose, telling her where to find him? Don't tell me that it is. I wouldn't believe you if you, on your knees as you are, was to swear it until you were black in the face!" And the over-cunning rogue chuckled and laid a finger along the side of his nose.

Mr. Gurd, as already has been shown, was a cool man in times of desperation, and swift at discovering and availing himself of advantages unexpectedly offered. He took his cue at once from the burglar's blundering remark.

"No, no!" said he, with great anxiety,

and holding out his hands entreatingly. "I said what wasn't true, I had not read it; I was reading it when you took it from me. I can swear to the writing. Let me have just another look, my good fellow. Don't be hard on me, Mr. Blake."

"I'll see you hanged first," responded the good fellow, in triumph. "If you haven't read it, why so much the better for me; if you have—and, upon my soul, I believe that you have—I don't care a rap. I'll have first pull, let who ever will come after."

Mr. Gurd appeared as though in a frenzy of despair. "Look here," said he, "say that you will give me back that paper and I will pay you down five-and-twenty pounds now and a hundred more if anything is to be made by it."

But clever Mr. Blake shook his head. "You shall have it when I have done with it," said he; "I'll send it back by the tuppenny post. I'll be off at once."

"What! at this hour in the morning?" exclaimed the doctor, feigning unheard-of agonies of mind. "Why, you had better wait until the morning, my good sir; the keen air after your late hurt will do you more harm than you imagine. You will be laid on a sick-bed; you will, indeed. Let me persuade you, if you will not give me back the paper, at least to stay till the morning, and then, you know, we can——"

"Go together, eh? Thanky. I can find my way, I'll be bound," interrupted Mr. Blake, in the highest spirits. "Now, about the money."

"What money?"

"Money for the job you engaged me on. Money for my sore shoulder, and for the loss of more blood than you've got in your wizened old carcass. Shall I make out a bill with the separate items set out, all regular, or shall we say a lump sum? I'd say a lump sum, if I was you. I should feel so preciously aggravated if I sat down to write about it that I should be sure to stick it on. Say a hundred pounds."

"A hundred what?" returned the doctor, in genuine alarm. "A hundred pounds for a scratch like that? Why, I'd stand up and let anybody make a target of all my limbs for the money. Tell you what I'll do. Give me back that paper, and I'll say fifty."

"I'll say fifty, but I won't give you the paper," remarked Mr. Blake, after a few moments of reflection. "It will serve my turn just now."

"It is villanous extortion; but I suppose that I must submit," observed the doctor. "I must give you a cheque unless you wait till the morning, and then you can have ready money."

But the burglar was exactly as obstinate as Anthony hoped he would be. The cheque was as good as ready money, he said, since, if it wasn't paid at the bank, it would be easy to bring it back to the pill-shop. So, stepping down into his room, Mr. Gurd presently returned with a cheque for fifty pounds sterling, payable to "Mr. Tomkins," and handed it to the burglar, after which, finding further persuasion for Mr. Blake to prolong his stay till daylight unavailing, he assisted him on with his jacket, and even lent him a silk neckerchief, his own being saturated with blood, and accompanying him, without noise, to the street-door, there took leave of him.

"It is a long game," muttered Dr. Gurd, as, with an almost cheerful countenance, he closed and fastened the door; "but I hold good cards, and I think that I shall win yet."

"She must not go to Dyot!" said he, as he crept up-stairs to the garret. "This precious paper scrap is of no more use than a pebble if that is allowed. She must be kept safe—for a while, at least, until I have made my market with this ship-robbing ruffian. She might be kept up here!"

The window of the garret was a perched-up window, so high that, standing on the ground, a grown person could do no more than peep through the bottom panes of it. Outside the window were the leads of a gutter that ran the entire length of the row of houses of which Mr. Gurd's was one.

It was possible that thieves might creep along this gutter and gain admittance through the window; and to guard against such a calamity iron bars had been fastened across and across on the inside. Mounting on a chair, Mr. Gurd felt and shook these bars carefully, and with perfect satisfaction, judging from the expression of his countenance. Then he examined the door. There was no lock on it, but a big, old-fashioned iron bolt fixed mid-way; and about this, after a little reflection, the doctor went to work like a journeyman carpenter.

The only tool he required besides the screwdriver that lay handy was a gimlet, and such an implement formed part of his economical pocket-knife. It was a tough job taking off the old bolt, for the screws were long and rusted in; but with perseverance he managed it. It was destined for fixing *outside* the door. A quarter of an hour saw this latter operation completed; and then the doctor, having prepared the cage, retired to his own room till the bird was stirring.

CHAPTER X.

MARY KETTERING FROM HER WINDOW WITNESSES A PANTOMIME.—LOCKS, BOLTS, AND BARS.

OTHER considerations besides those that Mr. Gurd had urged had resolved Mary Kettering to defer her departure from Old Fish Street until the further advance of morning.

Her position was one of considerable difficulty. Should she go home—home to Kensington, that is? As it appeared, she had discovered all that was to be known concerning the fate of her child. She had succeeded even beyond what she could reasonably have expected had the lamentable circumstances attending the case been previously made known to her—she had secured the precious relic, baby's tiny black curl. This was worth all the risks and hazards she had encountered since she fled from her father's house. Were the dangers and the ultimate reward again set before her, she would do as she had done once more without hesitation. But how could she go home declaring that the object of her formidable undertaking was achieved with nothing more to show in proof of her assertion than this poor little scrap of hair? In all probability, her abrupt departure from her father's roof was looked on as the step naturally ensuing on what she knew was regarded as the fatal first, and as establishing beyond question her inclination for depravity. How, under such circumstances, could she face her parents—her tearful old mother, her father, with all his ripe-hearted love for her curded to sourness and bitterness? Least of all, how could she undertake such a mission in the night? If it was to be done at all, it must be by honest daylight and with an honest and undoubted advocate as her companion.

Such a one she hoped to find Mr. Dyot. He was an honourable man—a man of goodness and piety; and he had promised to help her.

She could go at once to the address at

Stangate that Mr. Dyot had given her; but since, as was evident, the suspicions of Anthony and his sister were aroused, they would probably follow her. Even if she succeeded in eluding their vigilance, it was not improbable that a visit to Mr. Dyot at three in the morning might not only cause him annoyance, but lead to inconvenient curiosity on the part of the good folks with whom he had newly taken up his abode. Besides, as it seemed to her, no harm could arise from her prolonging her stay at the doctor's house yet a few hours. So long as she remained in the room that overlooked the street she need not fear personal violence from her enemies, to say nothing of the good will of her friend the burglar. To be sure, he had not in as many words declared "don't be afraid, young woman; you may depend on me; any moment between this and daylight I'm your faithful watch-dog, lying wide-awake, ready to fly to your assistance at your slightest call;" but he had looked it most emphatically, and, as before stated, she was grateful for the tacit assurance, and relied on it not a little.

But, judge of her alarm and amazement

when, as she stood sadly at the window gazing out on the cold, grey morning (Mercy, finding all her persuasions and wiles of no effect towards inducing the young woman to exchange so much as a single word with her, had retired spitefully to her bed-room, leaving the door wide open, however), Mary, after some little noise and whispering on the stairs, heard the front door open, and saw her faithful watch-dog stealing off down the street in apparently a perfectly contented way. That he had not strode out of the house without the consent and knowledge of the doctor, how could she doubt, for she had heard the whispering, and the sound of Mr. Gurd's footsteps creeping back to his own room after the burglar's departure. But this was not the most astonishing part of the affair.

As, looking from the window, she watched the friendly burglar, he suddenly paused and looked back, and, catching sight of her, as it seemed, crossed the road just opposite the house, and, first looking carefully to the right and to the left to make quite sure that nothing in the shape of a constable was in sight, proceeded to the performance of a pantomime most inexplicable. Taking from an inner pocket what in the dim light might have been a card or a letter, he held it up to her, pointed it at himself, and then extended it vigorously and with great earnestness in a westerly direction; after which he replaced the mystery in his pocket, shook his head both negatively and affirmatively, with a rapidity that was of itself bewildering to contemplate, and concluded by raising his hat gallantly, laying his hand on his heart devoutly, and kissing the tips of his fingers impudently. Then he was off and away in an instant.

What could he mean? It was scarcely likely that the villanous doctor had won him over to act against her, or why should he take such pains to make her understand that he was still acting, if not absolutely in her behalf, at least in a manner that could not occasion her displeasure even. What was she to infer from his exhibition of the card or letter, or whatever it might be? For a moment the suspicion crossed her mind that it might have to do with Mr. Dyot's whereabouts, but when the robber so emphatically indicated an almost opposite direction to that in which the fugitive might be discovered as the one to which the paper related, the alarm vanished immediately.

Mercy, lying on her bed with her clothes on, witnessed Mary's agitation without suspecting the cause.

"Come away from the window, can't you, you obstinate fool?" said she; "it is growing towards daylight now, and people will see you as they pass."

It was not likely. One of her promised protectors having failed her, her chief safeguard was to remain at the window; and there she stayed, drawing the curtain, however.

There she stayed, wondering and pondering, and almost frozen with cold, poor little woman, until the day advanced, and business abroad began to stir. Then said she to Miss Gurd, "Give me the key to unlock the door, if you please; I will go now. Let me go up to my room and pack my things."

Mercy, however, did not comply with this modest request. Through the small hours of the morning she had lain distracting her brain with vain imaginings as to what her brother Anthony was doing all this time; whether she fully understood the glance he had given her, and whether he *had* as yet made any move in connection with it, and again whether—and this was the most dismal speculation of all—if he had made any move it would turn out to be a clever and useful move, or if, according to his luck of late, he had again burnt down his piggery in order to roast his porker, as the country saying is. Where was brother Anthony now? What was he doing?

"I will go up with you," said she, in reply to Mary's request. "I always make it a practice when my servants leave me to overlook the packing of their boxes. You will excuse me, but even your unexceptional behaviour does not incline me to break through the rule."

"You are welcome to search my box, ma'am," returned Mary, resolved that it should not be her fault if there was another "scene" before she left the house; "you will, I promise you, find nothing in it but what belongs to me." And this she said fearlessly, although she had it fair in her mind that the little black curl was there bestowed.

"We shall see," replied Miss Gurd, prolonging the process of dressing as much as possible, so as to increase the probability of her brother being up and about when she ventured out of the room. She need not have troubled herself on this head, however. Since the time when his little job of bolt fixing was completed, Anthony had been counting the minutes; and as he heard his sister's door open he came down the stairs, looking anything but like a man who had passed a refreshing night, although he had partaken of his customary cold bath, and wore a clean shirt in lieu of the blood-bedabbled one he appeared in when last seen.

"Good morning, my love! are you better?" exclaimed Mr. Gurd, addressing his sister, and affecting a degree of composure that the nervous twitching of his mouth gave the lie to.

"She's going, now," rejoined Mercy not heeding her brother's affectionate inquiry; "she is going up to see to her box. You had best come up too."

"Certainly, my dear; if the young woman insists on going, we can have no interest in keeping her. I need not remark, however, that since she chooses to leave us in this sudden manner, causing us an amount of inconvenience that she has no idea of, the money she deposited with us is forfeited."

"I am willing to go without my money —for the present, at all events," replied Mary, who was only anxious to be gone.

Anthony, going first, reached the top landing and entered Mary's room a step or so in advance of his sister and Mary, there arrived, he stood with his back to the door, that opened inwards, so concealing from view the transferred bolt.

"Come in," said he to Mary, "it is all right, I dare say, only it is a rule with us, you see." At the same time, by a motion of his hand, he signalled to his sister to stay outside.

There was her box, apparently just as she had left it, and without the least suspicion, Mary entered and approached it. Then, swift as thought, Mr. Gurd banged to the door and shot the bolt into the stout hasp screwed on to the door-post.

Too startled and amazed to utter any cry, Mary stood for several seconds motionless, and then, the terrible truth occurring to her, she raised the lid of her box, and, with desperate haste, bundled its contents out on to the ground. The discovery of one of her losses—that of the poor gentleman's address—was less shocking, because it was to that her sudden suspicion pointed. But it was not until the box was right empty, save for the packet of old love-letters and a few other trifles, that her great loss was revealed to her—the loss of all that remained to her of her darling curly-headed baby smuggled from her side and so cruelly murdered. Then she cried out with a vengeance. Springing at the door with the fury of a trapped tigress, she shook it hard, at the same time screaming out to her jailers to give her back what they had robbed her of—begging, demanding, and threatening in a breath. But, so long as the bolt held, Mr. Gurd did not mind a jot how loud she squealed, well knowing that the upper rooms of the houses on each side of his were used as warerooms, and that there was little danger of a woman's voice being heard beyond their thick walls.

"Pray, what does all this mean, Tony?" his sister demanded, when she had sufficiently recovered from her astonishment to speak.

"It is all right, my dear. I've done the trick this time, I think;" and the doctor rubbed his hands with self-satisfaction.

"But where is *he?*"

"What, that scoundrel Blake? Gone! Done! Diddled beautifully, and put on the wrong track!"

Not a word about the fifty pounds, however.

But Mercy shook her head. She had seen her brother in raptures before, and had known him reduced, after all, to the ignominious necessity of paying the piper. It seemed a strange step towards smoothing away difficulties, this act of forcible incarceration.

"Come down-stairs," said she; "we had better have an explanation of this before the matter goes too far."

First carefully examining the bolt-hasp with a satisfactory result (Mary's cries had considerably subsided during the above-narrated whispered conversation), Mr. Anthony accompanied his sister to the apartment below.

"Light the fire," said he; "I think that I've found something that had best be burnt at once."

"A rare find, if it's good for nothing but burning," rejoined Miss Gurd, ungraciously (she had by this time made up her mind that Anthony really *had* burnt down his piggery to secure a little roast pork); "let me see it."

"First of all, what do you think of this?"

"Dyot's address, no doubt; I can swear to the writing," returned she; "but how will it be the better for burning?"

"No, no; that must be kept," replied Anthony, eagerly repossessing himself of the precious scrap, and depositing it in the recesses of his pocket-book. "This is what had best be burnt, if I am not greatly mistaken. It's one of the queerest things I ever heard of."

And he produced Mrs. Craven's last letter, containing the little black curl.

Mercy, although perplexed, was decidedly disappointed.

"What's there queer in that?" asked she, sharply. "You knew all about it months ago. I showed it you when I received it."

"To be sure you did. But how came it in her box?"

"In her box, hey?" Mercy, too, evidently began to see something queer about the matter. She took the letter in her hand, and, turning it over, made a discovery that had escaped her brother. This was the pencilled notes of the conversation that had long ago taken place between her brother Anthony and Billy Hogan, the sailor.

"Upon my word," said she, "we have been sitting on the edge of a pretty sort of volcano since that hussy has been here. No wonder that she was so thick with him! No wonder that he was so suspicious of our doings against him! It is time that we shut up shop, Tony, when we find ourselves beat by a chit such as she is." And

Miss Gurd strode up and down the room in a very wrathful mood.

Mr. Anthony, stooping to light the already-laid fire, paused, with the match in his hand, and inquiringly looked up as his sister uttered these last words.

"Thick with him?—thick with Dyot, do you mean?"

"Who else?" replied Mercy, snappishly.

"Why, you never mean to say that *he* was the child's father!"

"You are talking like a madman," exclaimed his sister, after regarding him in amazement; "what has a child to do with it?"

The match burnt out in Mr. Anthony's hand, unapplied to the combustibles in the grate.

"Upon my word, I begin to think that I *am* a madman, Mercy, my dear," said he, "if you are talking sense, that is; for I can't make head or tail of what you are saying."

"Well, what about a child? Whose child did you suppose that I meant that Dyot was the father of?"

"Why, Mary Kettering's child, to be

sure; you remember—the old harness-maker's daughter, that——"

Mercy interrupted him with an exclamation of impatience. "The best thing that you can do is to go to bed," said she. "What has the wench at Kensington to do with this confounded business? What can she know either of Dyot or the designing baggage up-stairs? Answer me that."

"So I can, in half a dozen words—the designing baggage up-stairs and Mary Kettering are one and the same person, if I am not most confoundedly out in my reckoning," replied the doctor, spitefully.

One would have thought that it was Miss Gurd who was taking leave of her senses now, judging from the helpless manner in which she sank down on to a chair, staring at her brother.

"Kettering's daughter and this one the same!" she exclaimed, in a low voice; "who told you that, Tony? How do you know?"

"Nobody told me, or I shouldn't have believed it; but after what I've discovered, it's as plain to me as that you are alive before me." And then Anthony proceeded to explain to his sister the peculiar circumstances under which he had found the torn letter cover bearing the address of the harness-maker at Kensington.

Mercy said nothing in reply. What her brother had told her lifted the curtain from before a prospect so full of trouble and perplexity that all she could do was to sit staring at it, as it were in helpless amazement.

"But what did *you* mean when you spoke of the volcano we had been sitting on ever since this girl has been in the house?" pursued Anthony; "what is it that accounts for her being so thick with Dyot?"

By way of reply his sister handed him Mother Craven's letter, pointing out the pencil memorandum concerning Master Hogan's account of the wreck and the treasure as she did so. That completed the picture.

CHAPTER XI.

MR. BLAKE UNDERTAKES A JOURNEY TO KENSINGTON.—AN ACCOUNT OF HIS UNEXPECTED RECEPTION BY AN INHABITANT THEREOF.

MR. GURD was quite correct in his conjecture that the deluded Mr. Blake would make hot haste to Kensington.

At the time when the burglar took leave of the little doctor, it was too early to start, however. What he intended doing, and what he made such ridiculous endeavours to convey to Mary Kettering as being his intention, was first to hasten home to Spitalfields to the relief of the anxiety of Micah his brother, and such other of his friends as took an interest in his welfare; to put himself in decent condition as regarded his habiliments, and then to betake himself to the address on the paper, making the best of matters, not only for himself, but her as well, as he gallantly expressed in the manner before described.

Nor must too much credit be awarded the robber for his promptitude in arranging to his satisfaction a means by which the present illegal holder of Captain Crosbie's treasure—" worth a hundred small fortunes"—might be compelled to disgorge a portion of the enormous booty. It must be borne in mind that such a scheme was an old affair with Mr. Blake, dating, as to its origin, indeed, from the evening when the sailor, Hogan, had been so obligingly communicative in the tavern-parlour at Ratcliff; and since that time it had been wrought more and more towards what the brothers Blake regarded as perfection. All that was wanting was a knowledge of the intended victim's whereabouts, and now that this was provided, the work was quite easy.

About ten o'clock that morning a coach halted at the door of the decent little shop in the High Street, over which was inscribed " Kettering, Harness-Maker," and Mr. Blake, disguised with false whiskers, and genteely attired, and with his arm in a sling, alighted therefrom.

It must be confessed, however, that when the little shop is described as decent looking, that is the extreme of the degree of praise that may be bestowed on it. It was not, alas! what it used to be. Time was, and not so very long ago, either, when Kettering the harness-maker's was the sprucest shop in the row. At the door-posts hung saddles and bridles with their gay furniture of silver-plate, while the interior of the window was resplendent with handsome whips and saddle-cloths of many colours, and bits and buckles, shining so in the sun that it made one wink to look on them; while the lord and master of all, with his white shirt sleeves rolled back, exposing his muscular arms, and his white bib apron, and his jolly prosperous-looking face, hummed a tune as he busied himself over harness, old or new.

But now the aspect of affairs was sadly changed. A melancholy mantle of tarnish had descended upon the entire establishment—upon the silver mountings and the gay housings, upon the twinkling buckles and the splendid whips, suggestive of Rotten Row and the Mall. It had not even spared the harness-maker; indeed, it had begun with him, and spread around; and if ever there was a man tarnished from his original lightheartedness and joviality, that man was poor old Job Kettering. It was all through that "poor thing," as he now called her. The first shock was bad enough, but the second and last "did him up" completely. It did his wife up, to, poor soul! and that was worse than all. She couldn't stand up against it. She had been ailing a long time, and the discouraging discovery that Mary had gone with no more good-bye than was briefly written in a note, together with a vague intimation that she would come back "in better times," prostrated her so that they had to lift her to bed within a month, from thence to the coffin in which she was conveyed to the quiet retreat behind the grey old church hard by.

That is why old Kettering wears that wisp of black crape about his working cap. That is why his once bright eyes are now so dull, and his nose so like the nose of a drunkard. "Where is the use of standing up against it?" says the poor old chap. "If I had anything to fight for, I'd fight; but I haven't. Let me have another fourpenn'orth, hot, please, landlady."

As Master Blake alighted from the vehicle Job Kettering was sitting on the shop-stool, brooding, and with his arms folded. In the old time, seeing a gentleman alight from his carriage, he would have had the shop-door open briskly enough; but now he had lost his appetite for orders, and he kept his seat while Blake let himself in. Then he condescended to say,

"How can I serve you, sir?"

"Nothing in the harness way, thanky. I've not come to do business with you at all, in fact, but with a person residing here."

"A person residing here!" repeated old Kettering, rousing a little from his apathy.

"Ay; your name is Kettering, is it not?"

"My name is Kettering. There's nobody lives here but myself now, excepting old Betsy Harman, the charwoman; perhaps t's her that you want."

"Nobody but yourself and the charwoman, hey!" This denial of Mr. Dyot rather convinced Mr. Blake than otherwise that he was on the right track. Of course, after his persecution at Doctor Gurd's he would be careful to instruct his landlord to deny him to strangers.

"Nobody at all! What made you think otherwise?"

"Nothing short of certainty, my friend. In which part of the house does Mr. Humphrey Dyot live, pray?"

"Mr. Humphrey Dyot! Don't know such a person," replied the old harness-maker, gruffly. He didn't like the look of his customer, or his way of asking questions.

"Come, come; you act your part very well, but it won't do. P'r'aps if you knew who you was talking to you'd be a little more particular about speaking the truth. I've got the address in the gentleman's own writing, and I know that he is here. I am his friend. See, here is the address."

It was on old Kettering's lips to tell the speaker to be off for an impudent puppy before he was kicked out, when he caught sight of the writing on the paper that Mr. Blake held in his hand, and at once eagerly snatched at it; in a condition of excitement that struck the burglar as being not a little remarkable under the circumstances, he fumbled out his spectacles with a shaking hand, and adjusted them with anything but exactitude astride the bridge of his nose. He knew the writing instantly, as undoubtedly he would, since it was the performance of no other person than his elder brother, Joe, who lived down in Norfolk, and who had written to him some six months since.

"Where did you get this from?" exclaimed the old man, starting up from his stool with such violence that his spectacles fell to the ground. "Who gave you this?"

"Mind your own business, old gentleman," returned Mr. Blake, coolly; "you recognize it, it seems, wherever I got it from; and now perhaps you will be so kind as to——"

But he was not permitted to finish his observation. All unexpected and quick as thought the old harness-maker made a spring at him and caught him about the throat with his tough hands.

"You scoundrel," cried he, his eyes flashing and the veins in his forehead swelling big, "where 's my daughter? Wherever this came from there she is! Tell me, or, by the living God, I'll kill you where you stand!" And, releasing one hand from Mr. Blake's throat, Kettering caught up one of those queerly-shaped leather-cutting knives like those that cheesemongers use, and brandished it before the young man's eyes.

Half choked and bewildered as he was by the sudden attack, Blake knew not what to reply. Had he been sound in body it is not unlikely that the desperate old harness-maker would speedily have found himself worsted, for Blake was a powerful young man, and not over particular how hard or where he hit when his blood was up; but, weakened as he was, with his left arm quite useless, the best he could do was to catch the wrist of the hand with the knife in it and hold off that murderous weapon.

"I don't know what you mean, you lunatic!" he gasped. "What have I to do with your daughter? Will you take your hand from my throat before I make you?"

But old Kettering held on the tighter. "Where is she," cried he, in a voice that might have been heard on the other side of the way (where, by-the-by, was a livery-stable with half-a-dozen sturdy ostlers, doubtless obliging neighbours of the harness-maker, loitering about). "If you know nothing about her, and I can't believe she'd disgrace her old father for an ugly cur like you, you know who does; will you tell me where she is?" And, pressing forward with all his might, he capsized Mr. Blake over the work-board, and the two men came to the ground with a terrific clatter of working tools.

But Kettering was uppermost, strong as an old bull, and he still had Mr. Blake's windpipe under his thumb.

"I can't speak if you throttle me," said the burglar, feebly; "d'ye know you're attacking a man with a broken arm? If you want me to tell you anything, give me breath enough."

"Now speak, then," exclaimed the valorous old harness-maker, shifting his hand a little. "Where is she?"

"May I be struck dead this moment, if I know even who you are talking about," answered Blake, in all sincerity; "my business is with a man, not a woman. If you don't know anything about the man I want, and, upon my soul, I don't believe that you do, let me go; I never hurt you."

"Where did you get this from?" persisted Kettering, indicating the address which he had thrust into the bosom of his waistcoat, so that he might have both hands at liberty.

"If I tell you, will you let me go?" replied Blake, in no little alarm. There were a woman and three or four boys staring in wonder through the shop window.

"I won't promise; tell me first."

"Then I got it from a confounded old thief who keeps a doctor's shop in Old Fish Street. He may know about your daughter. Stay!" continued Mr. Blake, a light dawning on him; "your daughter, do you say? Is her name Mary?"

But before Kettering could answer, the door opened and the parish constable put his head in.

"What's the disturbance, Kettering?" said he; "is there anything I can do for you?"

Hearing his voice, the harness-maker let go his hold on Blake, who in the struggle had lost his false whiskers. The constable was a harmless man enough, and quite unlikely to recognize him; indeed, he had been installed in his office in consideration of his failing eyesight rendering him unfit to follow his trade, which was that of a ladder-maker. But Blake was in ignorance of this fact. His shoulder was crippled, but his legs were sound, and, suddenly darting out of the door, he was away, fleet as a hare.

"Is he a thief? Shall I go after him?" eagerly demanded the weak-sighted policeman. "What has he done?"

"Nothing that the law calls stealing," Kettering answered, exhausted by his late tremendous exertions, and sinking down to a seat; "let him go. Oh, if he has only told me the truth! If he has only told me the truth!"

Concerning the doctor resident in Old Fish Street, the poor old fellow meant. Had his wife been alive and present, she would at once have identified the Old Fish Street doctor as the man whose sister had charge of the unlucky little brat whose birth had caused all this mischief. But Kettering knew very little of the details of that unfortunate business, and he was not inquisitive on the subject.

He stored in his mind the words Mr. Blake had uttered, however, and, soon as the knot of idlers had dispersed from his shop, he put on his hat and took off his apron, and, bidding Mrs. Harman, the charwoman, inform all comers that he should probably return by dinner-time, he at once bent his steps towards that part of the town where Old Fish Street is.

It was not more than eleven o'clock when he arrived there, with no more definite guide as to whom he was looking for than "the doctor's." Old Fish Street, however, did not in those days abound in medical residents—indeed, the only red lamp visible from one end of it to the other was that exhibited by Mr. Gurd; and into Mr. Gurd's shop Kettering strode.

CHAPTER XII.

IN WHICH THE LION THAT WENT RAGING TO OLD FISH STREET IS SUBDUED, AND, BY THE WILES OF THE DOCTOR, IS CONVERTED INTO AN AGREEABLE TRAVELLING COMPANION.

MERCY was alone in the parlour behind the shop when the old harness-maker, pushing open the door with a vigour that set the little guard-bell which surmounted it dancing and singing at a tremendous rate, entered the pill establishment. Anthony was up-stairs, dressing to go out.

"I beg your pardon, ma'am," observed blunt Job Kettering, as Mercy advanced to receive his commands. "I beg your pardon; but do you happen to know any other doctor in this street, besides the gentleman that lives here!"

Miss Gurd had a keen memory for faces. She had seen this one but once before, but she immediately recognized it as Mr. Kettering's. To her great satisfaction, however, she at once perceived that he had no more recollection of her than if she had the day before arrived from Japan.

"There is no other doctor's shop in the street, that I am aware of, sir," replied she, with much civility. "Anything that you may require I have no doubt that we can supply you with."

"Well, since you are the only doctor's hereabouts, maybe you will be able to," returned the harness-maker, grimly. "My name is Kettering."

"Yes, sir," said Miss Gurd, unmoved to all appearance, as though he had announced his name as Brown or Snooks.

"Did you never hear of the name?" pursued the speaker, laying his hat and stick on the counter and seeking the fragment of letter-cover he had not neglected to bring with him. "Kettering, harness-maker and saddler, High Street, Kensington."

"I have so little to do with the affairs of the shop, sir, that it is not likely that I should know you or your name, if you were never so old a customer," returned the lady graciously. "If you will sit down for a few moments I will fetch my brother."

"Ay, that will be best, perhaps. Don't be long, ma'am, if you please, because my business is urgent."

Up-stairs flew Miss Gurd, the expression of her countenance dismally altering the moment it was turned from the customer in the shop; and unceremoniously burst in on Mr. Anthony, who at the moment was adjusting his highly-respectable white neckerchief.

"Here's more fat in the fire," she cried. "It's of your upsetting, and you had best come down and see about it."

"Why, what's the matter?" exclaimed Anthony, in dismay. "Come down and see to what?"

"Old Kettering, from Kensington is here—down-stairs in the shop, and has a pretty fair knowledge of how the matter stands, if the expression of a man's face goes for anything."

Mr. Gurd's own face instantly became as white as his neckcloth.

"In the shop!" he repeated, in dismay.

"How did you find out what he had come about?"

"Because he let it out, or as good, as soon as he opened his mouth."

"What did he ask?"

"He asked if this was the only doctor's in the street."

"Well, there wasn't much in that."

"And he asked me if I had ever heard of him—giving me his name."

"And why didn't you say 'No,' and send him about his business at once?" cried Anthony, fuming. "Instead of that, you told him that you did know the name, I suppose?"

"I told him that I should fetch you; and that's what I've come to do," replied his sister, maliciously. "What else could I do?"

"What—what sort of a man is he?" asked Anthony, after a pause.

"A square-built old fellow, with great hands," replied Mercy.

"Umph!"

"A determined-looking man; carries a stout stick."

"Ah! I wish you would go and tell

him that I am not at home, my dear," said Anthony, imploringly.

"I told him that you were at home. Be quick. You will have him up here else, if he has his suspicions. He looks just the sort of man."

"But what can *I* tell him?" Anthony exclaimed, stamping his foot. "I've been worried at such a rate lately that I haven't an idea left in my head. Where's the use of my facing him, with nothing to say for myself? To be sure, I might——"

And here Mr. Gurd, ever lucky at hitting on a means of escape when driven into a corner, paused, with one arm in his coat, and regarded his grotesque self reflected in the looking-glass with a thoughtful and puckered brow.

"I tell you what, Tony, you might——" began his sister.

"Thank you. Since you have kept your precious counsel so long to yourself, I'll contrive to do without it," interrupted her brother, scornfully. "I know what I'll do!" And his troubled eyes suddenly assumed an expression of radiance almost as he hastened to complete his toilet.

"What will you do, Tony?" inquired his sister, anxiously. "Tell me, and I will give you my opinion as to how it will work."

"Wait and see; and then, p'r'aps, if you've got a grain of good nature in you, you will congratulate me on the way in which it *has* worked," replied Anthony, with his usual amount of confidence in his own schemes.

Who but a despairing and desperate man could harbour a suspicion against the meek and proper old gentleman who, entering the shop, blandly inquired of the impatient customer what might be his business with him.

"My name is Kettering, sir," said the harness-maker, shortly.

"To be sure, sir; so my sister informed me."

"Do you know of any person of that name?"

"To my knowledge, I never was acquainted with a gentleman——"

"I didn't say a gentleman, sir. My business is not concerning a gentleman, but a——well, a lady, God help her! My daughter, sir." And here the poor old fellow for an instant raised a hand to his eyes.

"Ah, indeed! No, sir, I am equally ignorant of a lady of the name you mention. The fact is that we ourselves are in considerable distress at the present time on account of a lady, or rather I should say a working female—a servant-of-all-work, in fact. It is a sad thing, sir, when the—the quiet and felicity of a domestic hearth is——"

"What's the name of the person, the young woman you allude to?" interrupted Kettering, who, while Mr. Gurd was speaking, had risen from the shop-chair, his face betraying his eagerness.

"Marsh, my good sir—Mary Marsh. She——"

"It's a lie, her name is not Marsh, it is Kettering," cried the old man, in a voice that made the little doctor's heart thump against his waistcoat. "I was told she was here. Where is she? Where's this Mary Marsh, as you call her? See if she will deny her name to her old father."

"Her old father!" repeated Mr. Gurd, regarding the old gentleman's agitated face in well-affected amazement. "Why, now I come to look at you with more attention, my dear sir, I am almost convinced——why, Lord bless my soul, the likeness is perfectly remarkable!"

"Hang about the likeness, sir; where's my gal?" and old Kettering smote the counter with his stout walking-cane in a manner that made a paper of pills there lying leap with a semblance of vitality very foreign to their nature.

"Mercy," exclaimed the little doctor, going to the foot of the stairs; "just step down here for a moment."

"Detect the likeness," he whispered, rapidly and meaningly to the lady in question, as she thrust her head over the stair rails above.

"You didn't know this gentleman when first you saw him, my dear?" remarked the doctor, when, in innocent obedience to his summons, his sister made her appearance.

"I did not observe him very particularly," returned Mercy.

"Do so now, then, my love? and tell me whom he reminds you of."

Chafing and fuming against such treatment, had Mercy conscientiously replied, it would have probably been to the effect that the gentleman reminded her of nothing so much as one of those elderly patients who occasionally applied to her brother for the extraction of a raging tooth; having the cue, however, she appeared to be instantly struck by the extraordinary resemblance, and exclaimed,

"The girl's father!—the same mouth—the same eyes—the same——oh! it is terrible!" and then conveniently concealing her eyes with her hands, Miss Gurd retreated to the little back parlour.

"What makes it terrible?" demanded old Kettering. "What have you done with her? Is she, too, dead, like her mother? I wish to God she had died when she was as little as the cause of all this trouble!"

"No, no, my good sir, she's not dead," remarked Mr. Gurd, soothingly; "she was well enough when we last saw her."

"And when was that?" eagerly asked Kettering.

"No longer ago than last evening."

"And where is she now?"

"Gone away, sir. She must have gone

in the night, when we had retired to rest, and the house was quiet."

"We only suspect that," spoke Mercy from the parlour; "she may have gone early this morning."

"And where has she gone? Have you no clue, no suspicion?" And then, as though it suddenly occurred to him, old Kettering continued, "who was that scoundrel that came to my house this morning?"

"The scoundrel that came to your house, my dear sir!" exclaimed Anthony, acting the wondering man to perfection; "really it is impossible for me to say. Pray what reason have you for supposing that I could give you any information as to who the person was?"

"Because he it was who told me that I might find my daughter here. He told me that after I had nearly choked him, the villain! But that's nothing to the purpose. Where's my daughter? That's what I've come here to find out."

"You'll excuse my remarking that it is a great deal to the purpose what this visitor of yours told you respecting me or my affairs," returned Mr. Gurd, with an offended air. "I may tell you, sir, that, as a humane man, as a man with a sister, sir, and a decent regard for the welfare of womankind, I may be willing to interest myself in restoring to her friends this unhappy young female; but I really must be permitted to protect myself as far as possible from the calumnies of my enemies. Pray what sort of person was this who called on you?"

Poor old Mr. Kettering was completely taken in by the impostor. He was a blunt, plain-spoken man himself, and it was difficult for him to understand how virtuous indignation could be so counterfeited. Besides, as well as he could make out, it was pretty evident that if he wanted intelligence respecting his daughter it would be as well to adopt a more pacific tone. So, apologizing for his display of temper, he simply recounted to the doctor the particulars of his interview and battle with Mr. Blake, and in support of his statement produced the torn letter-cover.

"Now I understand certain matters that were hitherto mysterious to me," remarked Mr. Gurd, as the harness-maker finished his narration. "The fellow did not tell you any more concerning himself than you have told me?"

"I have told you word for word, as well as I recollect; no more nor no less," returned Mr. Kettering. "Yes; there is something else to tell you: he came disguised, and left a pair of false whiskers behind him."

"Precisely; just what one might expect from so desperate a ruffian," remarked Mr. Gurd, with a meaning look at his sister, who had once more come into the shop, curious to hear the details of Mr. Blake's encounter with the harness-maker, and only sorry that the latter had not strangled him outright. "It was the whiskers that bothered me in identifying him. You will be astonished to hear, sir, that the man who called on you this morning is one of the most accomplished thieves in London."

"Not a bit astonished; not the least in the world, sir," returned Kettering, emphatically. "He looked it, every inch of him. I am only astonished that such a ruffian should know aught of me or mine."

"That is the saddest part of the story, my dear sir," said the brazen-faced old sinner, casting his eyes towards the ceiling. "I can understand your feelings as a father, and it pains my heart to be compelled to tell you that I believe your daughter—if she is your daughter—is lamentably inclined to bad company."

"I suspected as much," returned old Kettering, bowing his bald head on to his hands; "but such company as thieves and robbers! I wish to the Lord she had never been born, or that I had been laid beside her dead mother ere this cursed day dawned."

"Mind, I only speak from surmise," remarked the doctor, hastily; "for all that I know to the contrary, positively, she may be as good a girl as when she left your roof. It is my duty to tell you all that I know respecting this poor young creature. She came to us in answer to our advertisement some three months since, declaring that she had neither home nor friends, and imploring us to take her as servant. It was not prudent, I admit; but, as you doubtless are aware, my dear sir, there are times and seasons when the dictates of the heart are deaf to the promptings of reason; and we listened to her entreaties and bade her welcome, though the large number of seven-and-twenty applicants, all with unexceptionable characters, and some of them with money security, crowded this shop, waiting a hearing. Well, sir, her conduct, excepting that she insisted on receiving letters —which I must inform you, is against our rule—was, for the first month, all that could be desired. Then we began to suspect that she had made questionable acquaintances, from the fact of observing the fellow of whom you have been speaking, lurking about our house and endeavouring to get a word with her. But that is not the most remarkable part of the melancholy story. You must know, sir, that until very recently, we had as a lodger a gentleman named Dyot."

"Ay, Dyot!" remarked the old man, eagerly; "that was the name. Go on."

"An eccentric gentleman of some means," continued Mr. Gurd; "and, as it seems to us, encouraged by him probably, she conceived a partiality for him, and, in order to accomplish her ends, whatever they were, she resorted to all manner of mean devices to create a breach in the good understanding that had all along existed between our lodger and ourselves. Much as it grieves me, sir, to say as much to you, her father, she did not hesitate to insinuate to him that he was in danger of being poisoned. The consequence was that he went away from us without the least notice, and within a few hours she followed."

"How do you mean followed?" demanded Kettering, something much more formidable than tears gathering in his eyes.

"Followed him, I apprehend," returned the doctor, with a shrug of his shoulders. "It is a sad conclusion to arrive at; but, regarding the matter fairly, and from all points, I should say it was the most feasible."

Old Kettering nodded, as though he thought so, too. After a few moments of reflection, however, he again shook his head—this time negatively.

"Feasible enough, as far as it goes; and only as far as it goes," said he, sadly.

"How much further would you have it go, sir?" returned Mr. Anthony.

"I would have it go the length of making me understand the purport of that ruffian's visit to me this morning. I can't see its connection with my poor girl and this Dyot; can you?"

"To be sure I can; and so will you, I am sure, when I give you my view of it," replied the doctor, briskly. "Don't you see: the first rascal—Blake is his name, I believe—finds himself cut out of your daughter's regards by the second rascal—Dyot, that is; and the former finally discovers—by what means the devil, who has the conduct of such matters, only knows—that Dyot and the young woman have both left my house at pretty much the same time. Then, my dear sir, in steps jealousy. Actuated by passion and a yearning for revenge, this Blake seeks high and low for his rival; and, somehow getting hold of your address, he comes to you, under the impression, probably, that when they ran away from here, or, possibly before, they had got married, and that under such circumstances you would not unlikely be reconciled with your daughter, and be able to inform an inquirer where her husband might be found. That, I think, is as clear as clear can be. What do *you* think, sister?"

Anthony could not forbear making this appeal to Mercy. The arguments that he had used struck him as being so exceedingly ingenious, considering, of course, that they were quite unpremeditated and unprepared. Mercy admired them without doubt, but her admiration in its nature partook somewhat of that of a person who finds himself in the midst of a magnificent spectacle of blazing fireworks, and is in momentary expectation of being felled to the earth by a descending rocket-stick. So she contented herself by remarking that the case, as her brother put it, seemed very probable indeed.

Mr. Kettering thought so too, judging from the look of increased confidence he bestowed on the little villain.

"The only remaining question is," said he, "where has this Dyot gone? You have no clue to that, I suppose, my good sir?"

It was quite affecting to observe the

countenance of the simple-hearted Christian comforter as he made reply.

"My dear Mr. Kettering [here he took the old gentleman's hand], after the bad news it has been my unpleasant duty to convey to you, I am delighted to apprise you that the picture is not all darkness. I *do* know to where this imprudent young man has retreated. I may now tell you, and my sister can corroborate the assertion, that just as you came I was dressing to go out, the object of my journey being a visit to Mr. Dyot, that I might ascertain whether the young woman was really the guilty companion of his flight. That visit, sir, need not be deferred. You shall accompany me; and perhaps a father's stern demands may prove more effective than the entreaty of a friend."

"Lord Almighty bless you, sir!" returned the grateful old harness-maker, giving the doctor's hand a squeeze that made his eyes water in a singularly apropos manner. "I must confess to you that I came here expecting to find a designing ruffian, who, to suit his own rascally ends, kept my poor gal away from me. I beg your pardon a hundred times over, and yours too, miss. Shall we start at once, sir?"

Mr. Gurd was quite ready; and kissing his sister affectionately, at the same time favouring her with a wink that was intended to convey, "This is a rum start, don't you think? Don't understand it in the least, do you? Don't you say a word till you see how beautifully I'll work it," they set out together.

What an astonishing spectacle it would have afforded the old harness-maker's daughter could she have looked down from the window of her prison and seen her father hugging Mr. Gurd's arm so hopefully as they walked down the street!

CHAPTER XIII.

THE VISIT TO RUFFORD'S TERRACE—MR. DYOT MAKES A FALSE STEP, AND IS AT ONCE TRIPPED UP BY THE DOCTOR.

THE house in Rufford's Terrace, at Stangate, where Mr. Dyot had sought refuge from the designs of his enemies, was pleasantly situated on the verge of the river. The Thames lay in a clearer bed in those days than at present, and could rise of mornings without being nauseated by the sickening affluvia arising from the manufacture on its banks of gas, and soap, and bone manure.

Mr. Dyot's apartment was two stories high from the basement, and possessed a bow window, opening on to a balcony. At high tide the bright water rose abreast of the wall immediately beneath, and of nights could be heard softly beating against it in a manner peculiarly soothing to a weary mind.

Mr. Dyot's was a weary mind. Its self-imposed burden afforded it no rest, and day by day the weight increased, and each night as it came brought more ghosts—ghosts of the past conjured up for description in the terrible ledger—to haunt his sleepless pillow. There was no getting away from the monstrous thing—the ledger, that is. His soul had taken it to wife, as it were, and the two were one, and the hurt of one was the hurt of the other, and the neglect, and a single act of unfaithfulness was damnable, according to the solemn rites that ratified the marriage on that lonely island in the Indian seas.

For various reasons, not the least amongst them being his desire to avoid as much as possible all chance of his encountering his Old Fish Street enemies, Mr. Dyot had resolved that he would—at least, for the present—keep within doors, venturing out only for an hour at dusk of evening for a little necessary exercise. This morning, however, was an exception to the rule. It was necessary for him to go into the City on monetary business. He took all possible precaution, avoiding the road and hiring a row-boat at Lambeth Stairs to carry him to the neighbourhood of Tower Hill. The consequence was that he was from home when Mr. Gurd and his companion, Mr. Kettering, arrived at his residence; and great was his astonishment when he returned to find the two worthies in question seated in the hall awaiting his coming.

The impatient old harness-maker could scarcely be prevailed on by the wily doctor to refrain from asking questions of the lady of the house concerning his daughter, and was only persuaded to do so by Mr. Gurd's reminding him of the tact and ingenuity with which he had conducted the business so far, and how much better it would be to allow him (Anthony) to conduct the affair to a happy conclusion after his own method.

Soon, however, as Mr. Dyot, opening the outer door with his latch-key, made his expected appearance, the old man rose and confronted him without more ado. Pale as death itself was the poor gentleman's face at this sudden apparition of his enemy; and if, after Mr. Gurd's artful insinuations, anything was wanting to convince Kettering that the man before him was a robber of female chastity and a betrayer, it was by that circumstance provided.

"Where's my daughter, you scoundrel?" exclaimed the harness-maker, his stout walking-cane quivering in the grasp of his fist. "What have you done with her? Tell me this instant!"

"Really, my dear sir," interposed Mr. Gurd, who, for obvious reasons, was anxious that the scandal should be kept as snug as possible; "really, Mr. Kettering, I must beseech you to keep calm. Recollect your promise that you would do nothing rash. Besides, my good sir, it is as it stands a case of mere suspicion, and it is not impossible that this gentleman may be able to explain it away."

Mr. Gurd was spared the embarrassment of looking his victim in the face as he said this; his hungry eyes were fixed on the leather valise that the poor gentleman carried. He knew it again instantly.

"May I be permitted to inquire to what

I may attribute the honour of this visit ?" inquired Mr. Dyot, with all the calmness that he could assume, while at the same time he shifted the bag hanging from his hand, and put it under his arm.

"Where's my daughter, sir ?" again thundered old Kettering.

"Dear me !" Mr. Gurd nervously remarked, "this is very painful. May I trouble you to show us to your private apartment, Mr. Dyot, it will be better for us all, believe me."

Without a word in reply the poor gentleman led the way to the room, the window of which overlooked the river.

"Now, sir, if you will make your stay as brief as possible, you will oblige me," said he, severely, to the doctor. "Who is this person you have brought with you, and what does he seek here ?"

"What, for your sake, Mr. Dyot, I sincerely hope he will not find," replied Anthony, in a sadly respectful tone. "He seeks his daughter, sir. His name is Kettering, sir. He is the father of the unhappy young female who, as you are aware, was servant in my humble abode."

"*Was* servant! Where is she now?" exclaimed Mr. Dyot, in surprise and alarm.

Old Kettering laughed bitterly.

"You act very well, my fine gentleman," said he, "but it won't serve you. If she is not here with you, you know where she is, and you shall tell me before I leave this house." And down he sat in a chair, as a man determined that no abatement of his terms would suffice to move him from it.

"May I ask you, sir, who it was that informed you that I knew anything of your daughter?" said Mr. Dyot.

Too indignant to reply, the harness-maker indicated Mr. Gurd as his authority.

"I thought so. Now, sir, let me ask of you what this conduct means?" observed the poor gentleman, turning to the doctor. "What is it that actuates this persecution of an unoffending man—what do you hope to gain by it?"

"He has told me all about it; there is no use in trying to humbug me. I'm the wrong sort of man," interposed Mary's father.

"*Have* you told this person all about it?" asked Mr. Dyot of Anthony, regarding him meaningly.

"All, Mr. Dyot."

"All that *I* could tell?"

"Much more, my good sir; much more than you can possibly know," returned the daring doctor, unabashed.

"All about the attempted poisoning—all about the burglary? You drive me to this, Mr. Gurd."

"All about the poisoning as well as the projected burglary, my dear sir," returned Anthony, blandly, and turning to his companion for confirmation of his assertion, which was given without hesitation.

"Then am I to understand that this is a confederate of yours, sir?" exclaimed Mr. Dyot, when his amazement and indignation permitted him to speak. "Is this a friend of the man with whom you were overheard to be in rascally league against my life and property?"

"No. Mr. Dyot. The man you allude to, as I presume, is no friend of mine—Heaven forbid! He is, it is to be feared, an acquaintance of the misguided young woman who, as we have reason to suppose, stole away from my house with you—at least, she followed within a very few hours. It is owing to this last-mentioned circumstance that her father has waited on you this morning."

"But the fellow I mean was a housebreaker—a burglar," said Mr. Dyot, more and more bewildered. "You were heard conversing with him in the kitchen the night before I thought it prudent to escape from your abode."

"Indeed! Does the monstrous story take that turn amongst others?" returned the injured doctor. "And who, pray, was it that overheard me plotting with housebreakers and burglars?"

"Your servant, Mary—this person's daughter, as you say."

Mr. Gurd looked terribly shocked. "Good heavens! To think that so much cunning and depravity should lurk under so honest-looking a mask!" said he, turning to old Kettering. "It will, indeed, be a triumph, my good sir, if our endeavours to rescue this wretched young creature from the depths of vice into which she has been beguiled are crowned with success."

"You have heard what this gentleman says, sir," remarked Mr. Kettering. "She stole out of his house to follow you. What have you done with her?"

"I swear to you as a Christian man, and with a full knowledge of the awful doom that must surely overtake any one that dare trifle with the name of God, that since I quitted this man's house I have neither seen nor heard from your daughter, if so she is," responded Mr. Dyot, solemnly. "You, sir, are a stranger to me; and, if you really are what you seem, your distress may incline you to disbelieve me; but let Mr. Gurd tell you if, from his knowledge of me, I am likely to say or do a dishonest thing."

Mr. Gurd, by way of reply, shrugged his shoulders, and, crossing the room, looked attentively out of the window.

"That is no answer, sir," said Mr. Dyot, impatiently.

"I would rather that you did not press me on that point, Mr. Dyot," said Mr.

Gurd, still with his face to the window; "at least, before a third party."

"But I insist on pressing it," urged the poor gentleman, with passionate vehemence.

"If you insist I shall be compelled to yield," returned Anthony, now turning about, and with the face of a coward who is about to do a desperate thing. "Let me persuade you, Mr. Dyot, if for the sake only of our old friendship, to refrain from doing so."

"I do insist, fearlessly. I beg your pardon, however; perhaps you are right in opining that it was not the act of an honest man to come away from your house in the way that I saw fit to do. I think, however, that I am correct in my calculation that I owed you no money?"

Mr. Gurd approached the table, clearing his throat as he came.

"You just now remarked, Mr. Dyot, that I drove you to make certain accusations against me; it is now for me to retort in the same terms. As to your hasty departure from my house, that concerns me not at all since it seemed right to you.

You came to suit yourself, and I presume you left for the same reason. It is nothing to me, apart from moral considerations, that you allowed yourself to be imposed on by this person's daughter, taking her for what we took her to be—a simple-minded, virtuous young woman; whereas, as it is pretty plainly proved, she has for some time been the associate of individuals of known bad character. I will even go so far as to say that if you allowed your grosser feelings to govern you, and, misled by her selfish wiles, allowed yourself to become enamoured of this girl—nay, do not interrupt me—and entertained a design to take her away from the shelter of our roof—still, from a worldly and business point of view, it is nothing to me beyond the temporary inconvenience it subjects me to. But when this running off in the night—this absconding—somehow or another involves a loss to me of property to the value of a hundred pounds and more, why, then, I say it is more to me than I can afford to pass over in silence. You will pardon me, Mr. Dyot. It is a delicate matter, and I would have spared you its discussion before a third party, had you permitted me."

For a moment the poor gentleman had nothing to say; the insinuation conveyed in the doctor's last lengthy speech took away his breath almost as well as his power of utterance.

"This is news to me," spoke old Kettering, new alarms disturbing him; "you never mentioned a word of this before."

"I am aware of it, my good sir," returned Mr. Gurd; "I had compassion for your distress, and was loth to increase it. Such is the ugly fact, however."

"Let us come to a more perfect understanding," Mr. Dyot at length said. "Do you suspect this poor girl of robbing you of the property in question?"

"Nay, what I say is this," said Anthony, gaining courage now that the ice was broken; "property, consisting of jewels and trinkets, were deposited in a drawer in the parlour behind my shop—old family relics, that were never used and seldom looked at—have been stolen; and coupled with that circumstance is this other one—two persons, resident in my house, suddenly, and in the night, decamp from it. These two persons, I need not remark, were the young woman and yourself."

Mr. Dyot was a reformed man. For many months he had eschewed the ways of the world, the flesh, and the devil; and had adopted a form of religion that was fanatical in its severity; but the old Adam was not entirely ousted out of him yet. Rising from his chair he seized the little doctor by the collar with a grip that brought the blood rushing to his pale face.

"Dare you accuse *me* of anything so vile, you villanous trafficker in poison?" cried he. "Unsay what you just now uttered, or I shall be tempted to throw you through the window into the river."

But even under these untoward circumstances the doctor, driven to desperation, did not lose his presence of mind. His face was close to Dyot's, as the latter threatened him, really looking as though, on the slightest further provocation, he would be as good as his word.

"Dare I accuse *you?*" whispered he, grinning 'ragefully. "Why not? Who are you that are so high above suspicion? *What sort of tale could that bag tell?*"

CHAPTER XIV.

MR. GURD BENEVOLENTLY COMPROMISES A FELONY, AND, HAVING HOBBLED HIS VICTIM, DEPARTS REJOICING.

THERE is nothing like striking your iron while it is hot.

It was evident to Mr. Gurd's comprehension that by that last splendid stroke of his he had trapped his victim into a confession of his great secret scarcely less explicit than spoken words. "What sort of tale could that bag tell?" had been his simple inquiry, and straightway his late lodger had caught up the receptacle in question with an eagerness that was as easy to account for as that two and two make four. At last, after so many slips and tumbles, he had succeeded in climbing to the bough where the nest with the golden eggs was; and, without doubt, it would be his own fault now if he did not take it. His good luck nearly took his breath away. There was the treasure, the precious mystery of the wrecked merchantman, that in value exceeded "a hundred small fortunes" before his eyes—in his power.

"Have you anything else to say," presently remarked Mr. Dyot, still hugging the leather bag as though it contained his soul, and regarding the doctor as though he were the father of evil come in quest of it.

"If I have not said enough I have more to say," returned Anthony; "will you hear me now, or wait a more fitting opportunity?" And he glanced at Mr. Kettering, intimating that possibly a more fitting opportunity would present itself when that gentleman had taken his departure.

"Say on," said Mr. Dyot; "I have been guilty of nothing that I am anxious to conceal—from you and this person, that is."

"Perhaps not, my fine fellow," interposed the blunt harness-maker, who had, of course, observed the accused man's strange behaviour; "but it seems to me that appearances are against you. Look at your face in the glass, you villain! Is that the face of a man who is innocent, and has nothing to conceal? Out with it; you'd better, or you may find somebody else in the humour to talk about throwing people out o' window. Where's my daughter?"

Confound him, and his daughter, too! There was now a much more important move on the board than the idle discussion of where this blusterous old fellow's daughter was.

"Really, my good sir," the doctor observed, "I wish you would remain quiet, and leave the management of this unpleasant business to me. We are rapidly coming to an understanding—myself and Mr. Dyot; and nobody is to be thrown out of window, you may take my word. What do you say, Mr Dyot?"

"I say that you are a scoundrel," returned the person addressed, bitterly; "and, unless I am much mistaken, this poor man will presently find reason to tell you the same."

But old Kettering shook his unreasonable head. "It's no use you trying to come it over me in that way," said he;

"you'd better knuckle under. Why don't you answer this gentleman's question? What sort of tale could that bag that you take such precious good care of tell?"

"No tale that would interest you, my friend," returned Mr. Dyot, earnestly.

"True; *I* haven't lost a hundred pounds' worth of jewels. I've only lost my daughter," said Kettering; "maybe, however, that there are papers—letters in the bag that may be worth our reading. If you are an honest man, let us overhaul it." And the sturdy old fellow advanced with his hand extended.

Dyot had sunk down on to a chair, with his treasure in his arms; but as the harness-maker approached he leapt to his feet, looking dangerous.

"You shall kill me first," said he, eyeing his two visitors alternately, as though he wished them both to understand, without the least possibility of a mistake, that this was his settled determination.

Now, as may be readily imagined, this extraordinary behaviour on the part of the poor gentleman only added fuel to the hot fire of avarice that was already consuming

Mr. Anthony Gurd. It was awfully tantalizing to be obliged to dally with his prize when there was such a splendid chance of landing it, and all because this blundering old Kettering was present. Of course it would never do to readmit the fatal evil he had so recently escaped—a third finger in the pie.

"May I suggest a few words in private with you—out on the balcony, Mr. Dyot?" said he.

"I wonder that you have the daring to ask such a thing," replied Dyot, with a bitter laugh. "Possibly you are not aware that the tide is in, and that there are eight feet of water beneath the window."

Mr. Gurd shrugged his shoulders impatiently.

"There is, then, only one course to pursue, my friend," remarked he, turning to Mr. Kettering; "I am sorry that it is so, but he leaves us no alternative."

The old harness-maker heard the words, and the meaning they conveyed to his excited mind was that there was to be forthwith a forcible attack on Dyot to dispossess him of the suspected receptacle;

and, nothing loth, he nodded significantly and buttoned the top button of his coat.

"There'll be murder if you attempt it. Keep off!" cried Mr. Dyot, ghastly pale and catching up a heavy ruler.

"Tut! tut!" exclaimed the little doctor, holding up his hand in a manner deprecatory of all violence. "When a man has rights to enforce, his best friend is the law, my good sir. I have lost my goods, and, as you are witness, I have powerful reasons for supposing that they are concealed in that bag. You stay here and I will at once step out and procure the services of a constable."

"Do so," said Mr. Kettering; "no fear but that I'll keep an eye on him while you are gone."

It was cruel to drive him so hard, poor fellow.

"Stay!" exclaimed he. And Mr. Gurd, nothing unwilling, promptly returned to the room and closed the door.

"I am a wretched, miserable coward," continued the poor gentleman, hiding his face in his hands and groaning aloud. "This is the devil's work, I have no doubt;

but I have no strength to fight against him."

"A sanctimonious humbug!" growled old Kettering, under his breath.

"You might have saved yourself this pain, this humiliation, if you had at once adopted my suggestion, and let me had a word with you privately, Mr. Dyot," remarked Anthony, in terms of mild reproach.

"What do you say your loss is?" inquired Dyot, not heeding the doctor's last observation.

"Jewels—diamonds chiefly," returned the doctor, eyeing the bag wistfully.

"But their value?"

"About a hundred pounds. I can't say exactly."

"Will their value, instead of their restoration, satisfy you?"

Mr. Gurd shook his head dubiously.

"It is a ticklish matter to compromise a—ahem!—a felony," replied he. "I needn't remind you of what my duty is, sir. If I have reason to suspect that you have stolen property in your possession, be its amount great or small, the law demands that I shall make my suspicions known. Upon my word, I really don't know what to say."

"Don't you? It's plain enough," remarked the indignant harness-maker. "He has as good as confessed. Give him over to the law, and make no more bones about it."

"Exactly so, my dear sir," returned Gurd, who wished Mr. Kettering at Jericho; "but you will pardon my remarking that, although we may be compromising a felony, it may be only to enable him to screen a felon."

"What do you mean?"

"Only this: it might transpire, if we prosecuted the case, that it was your daughter that really committed the robbery."

Evidently this was a view of the case that had not occurred to the deluded old gentleman, and he looked as though he was sorry that he had spoken so vindictively.

"For God's sake let us make an end of this mockery," exclaimed Mr. Dyot, looking up with a painfully distorted face.

"You have me in the toils, don't prolong my misery."

"It would be unchristian to do so," returned Anthony; "and in reply to your previous question I will venture to say that I have no objection to money-compensation for my loss."

"A hundred pounds, that is."

"One hundred pounds, sir," replied the doctor. "I shall sustain a loss, I believe, but never mind — never mind. As you say, let us get this unfortunate business concluded."

"I have not as much money in the house," observed the victim, taking out his purse; "all that I have is fifty pounds —my allowance, as you are aware, for the coming half year—and that I drew from the bank this morning. Will you take that and my note of hand for the remaining fifty pounds?"

"Yes, I will," said Dr. Gurd, his amazing acuteness of perception leading him to suppose that his late lodger's anxiety was to make a seemingly simple arrangement before the inconvenient third party. Something within my breast seems to whisper to me that this terrible mystery may, after all, be cleared away; and I am willing to accede to the terms you propose, Mr. Dyot."

"Write me a receipt, then."

Mr. Gurd took a pen and dipped it in Mr. Dyot's ink-bottle.

"What had best be its form?" he inquired, hesitatingly; "it is rather a difficult document to indite. Shall I say for value received?"

"Give me a quittance of all demands on me, in consideration of a hundred pounds, received," replied Mr. Dyot.

"Of all *demands!*" returned the careful doctor, regarding the poor gentleman with a look of meaning that was quite lost on him; "Yes, it may safely take that shape, I think." And forthwith he wrote the receipt and pocketed the money.

"And pray how does this arrangement help me?" old Mr. Kettering not unnaturally inquired; "how much does it forward me towards finding my wretched child?"

"Ah! how does it help this poor man?" remarked the delighted Anthony, after a pause which he devoted to winking and otherwise dumbly telegraphing to the victim, who by this time he regarded as a confederate. "Come, come, Mr. Dyot, have you no grains of comfort to give to poor Mr. Kettering.

"I have some advice to give him that may lead to comfort," replied Mr. Dyot, made bold by possession of the receipt.

"Good! He will be grateful, I am sure," said the doctor, rubbing his hands.

"My advice is, that he avoid all dealings with you, who are both a hypocrite and a villain. I may mention this, however," continued he, turning to the harness-maker, "before I quitted this fellow's house, I gave to your daughter my present address, fearing what has, as it seems, turned out to be too true, that she might sooner or later be glad of a friend. I have not the least doubt, sir, that *as soon as it is in her power* she will communicate with me; when she does, you shall hear of it at once."

But Kettering could not trust him. He was not a man of deep penetration, and, from his observation of Mr. Dyot's behaviour, he was fully convinced in his own mind that the man of meek mien and pious speech was not only a canting humbug, but a consummate scoundrel and a robber. So impressed, he was about to declare himself in somewhat strong language when Mr. Gurd whispered him,

"Be silent. I have reasons for believing what he says; come away, and I will tell you what I mean."

"He may as well know what I mean, however," spoke Mr. Kettering, aloud. "Look ye here, Mr. Jewel-robber!" and he shook his big fist at him, "I shall wait at home until this time to-morrow. You may tell my bad daughter that if she comes home to me now—at once—I will take her in and provide for her, and save her from the devil if I can. If I don't hear from her or you by this time to-morrow, I shall be here again." And, so saying, he strode out of the room, followed by Mr. Gurd.

"Half a moment. I have left my umbrella," remarked the latter to his companion, when they were half way down the stairs. He found the poor gentleman with his face buried in his hands, just as they had left him.

"Well?" said he, looking up with a sudden start.

"Don't go out till dusk. I shall then return, and it will be your own fault if we don't arrange our little business on terms that are mutually satisfactory," spoke the doctor, rapidly; "and mind you *don't* go out, because the door will be watched." And, having secured his umbrella, he hastened away without awaiting an answer.

And as they left him, so he remained, hour after hour, quite downstricken by this new and unexpected misfortune. He did not appear to have left life enough in him to rebel against the inexplicable malice of Doctor Gurd, or to complain of his hard fate. Benumbed as a man under sentence of death, there he sat all the afternoon and until the evening shadows fell slanting across his window-blind. This seemed to rouse him from his apathy.

"He said that he would return at dusk," he muttered. "I must not see him; I dare not. I feel so against him that to meet him but once more would be to doom my accursed book to a bloody page. I will *not* meet him." And, probably the better to decide how the meeting might be avoided, he stepped out on to the balcony, where the evening breeze was blowing cool and refreshing.

It was quite dusk; and, looking abroad, he spied a waterman in his skiff, not more than forty yards distant, leisurely pulling up the stream and smoking his pipe, as a man whose day's work is done. The poor gentleman's course was decided at once. He called to the waterman and beckoned with his hand; and the man pulled in shore, finding bare room of water to float his skiff under the window.

"I will give you half a guinea if you will row me three miles up the river," he called down to the man, in a cautious whisper.

"Why, what's the matter, sir? Are the bailiffs after you?" asked the honest waterman, with a grin. In those days the sport of hunting debtors by means of the Cursitor Street kennel was much more popular than at present.

Mr. Dyot, not to utter a lie, nodded.

"Damme, get aboard, then. To bilk a bailiff I'd stand a pot o' beer, let alone earn half a guinea. Any luggage?"

"Only this bag. Can you catch it? Perhaps I had better lower it with a cord."

"Pitch it down. All right. It's rather a long drop for you, sir; but you won't drown if you fall in the water. It ain't more than eighteen inches, with a soft bottom."

"Pull your boat away, then."

Mud and water together, however, made a depth hip high for the fugitive to plump into. But there were no bones broken, and in two minutes he was aboard, and the jolly young waterman was pulling him up stream with a will.

CHAPTER XV.

IN WHICH THE MESSRS. GURD GO HARVESTING AND RETURN HUNGERING.

MISS MERCY GURD, sitting wearily watching in the little parlour behind the pill-shop, was glad enough, as you may be sure, to greet her brother on his return from Rufford's Terrace. Such had been her condition of mind, unsettled by her late indisposition and put to total rout and confusion by a succession of extraordinary and unaccountable events lately happening, that she would have felt immense relief at sight of him under even the most dismal circumstances. But, if appearance might be trusted, matters dismal were with Mr. Anthony things of the past. Never, except perhaps on certain rare occasions of conviviality, had his sister beheld him looking so cheerful and happy. Joy, it is said, is as intoxicating as wine, if the bounds of moderation are overstepped; and certainly it seemed that the little doctor had taken a cup of bliss too much. His little eyes sparkled like fire-flies, and he almost reeled as he raised the counter-flap, and, hurrying to Mercy, kissed and embraced her.

"It is all over, old gal," he exclaimed, in a voice quivering with emotion. "It has been a brisk, hot fight, and we have been floored in some of the rounds and hit while we were down; but they've knocked under, at last—thrown up the sponge and give in. Hooray!"

"Hush! You forget that we are not alone in the house," observed Mercy, convinced, by her brother's manner, that at least he had reasons for supposing that something wonderfully good had happened to him.

"No, I don't forget anything," returned Anthony, once more kissing his scraggy sister in the excess of his delight. "It is you who forget, you who are so mighty wide-awake and clever; it is me, the slow coach, you know, Mercy, my love, the woodenhead, the blunderer, who must think, and devise, and scheme, and make a fortune for himself and his sister. Ha! ha! Well, never mind; it is all over now. We'll forget all about our wranglings and janglings and live in clover."

"I wish you'd be a little steady, and tell me all about it from the beginning."

"Hang the beginning! It is the end I'm looking at—the end that justifies the means, you know, Mercy. Get me a cup of tea, there's a good soul. I feel as parched as an old acorn."

"Well, then, what is the end, Tony, if you will have it that way? Tell me what the end is." And she put her brother's joyously-dishevelled hair out of his eyes, coaxingly, and hastened to prepare tea, for she saw that his eyes were wandering to the cupboard where the brandy-bottle was.

"Diamonds is the end of it, jewels fit for a queen's crown. Gems worth a hundred—no, fifty—let's act fair and square to our friend: gems worth fifty ordinary fortunes. That's the end of it, my dear."

"Where are they?" inquired the practical Mercy.

"Where? Why, you don't suppose that

I've brought 'em away in my coat-tail pocket," replied Anthony, playfully. "No, my dear, the gentleman who has held possession of them so long consents to keep them yet a few hours longer. I'm to fetch them this evening."

"Who says so?"

"I say so. I might have claimed my share, and brought it away with me had it not been for that blustering old booby of a harness-maker who went with me. It wouldn't do, you know, to go too far before him."

"How far did you go, Tony?"

So he told her all about it from first to last, triumphantly exhibiting the fifty pounds and the note of hand for another fifty in proof of the extent to which the poor gentleman was in his power.

"And that isn't all," observed Anthony. "To be sure, the money shows something. It shows that Dyot has arrived at the conclusion that since matters have come to this pass between us, such a sum as a paltry hundred pounds is of no weight in the scale. But it was the way in which he looked at me that would have convinced you, could you have seen it; a savage, despairing look it was, that said plain as words, "D—n you! you've run me to earth; and I must yield, I suppose; there is no use in beating about any longer. We must divide the spoil, and I must make the best of it.'"

"But suppose he should decamp from his lodgings before the evening. What's to hinder him? I did not think of that," Miss Mercy observed, in sudden alarm.

"But I did," said her brother, with becoming pride; "I did, and provided against it. That pig-headed old saddler is on the watch. He's taking a bit of dinner at the 'Blue Anchor,' at the opposite corner of the street, and he has a fair view of the house where Dyot is from the window of the parlour. I'll wager that he don't take his eyes off the house till I go back. No fear of that; he's too mad after this precious daughter of his."

"I was just about to speak of her, Tony," remarked Mercy, looking grave. "What's to be done with her? She can't be kept a prisoner here."

"What do I care what comes of her? Soon as this little game I have in hand is played out, she goes packing. Let her go home to her father. How is she getting on?" he presently inquired; "have you heard anything of her since I have been away?"

"I haven't been up-stairs; I was afraid. I haven't been out of this room ever since you went away this morning."

"Well, it isn't worth while making a fuss, that I see, for the sake of a few hours, or I would go up to her," observed Anthony, as, crossing his legs comfortably, he sipped his tea. "I shall be back by eight or nine o'clock, and then she can go about her business if she likes. If we are obliged to pay a few pounds to keep her tongue still, why, we must. It will cost us something, no doubt; but we shall be able to afford it, thank heaven!"

And so the unlucky little villain amused himself, not only building his castle, but gilding and decorating it in the most gorgeous manner, and laying out the pleasure-grounds attached to it, until the day began to wane and it was time for him to keep his appointment with his victim. It was not difficult to discover, however, that, as the time for his departure drew nigh, he grew somewhat less confident in his demeanour.

"Would you take the pistol, if you were me, my love?" he asked his sister.

"I would if I thought that he meant violence, not without. You've done enough mischief already with that confounded thing." And Mercy shuddered as she conjured up the picture of the burglar bleeding at the foot of the stairs. "I understood you to say that you were convinced that he would come to terms as quiet as a lamb."

"It would be awkward if he was to turn round on me all of a sudden, my dear. It wouldn't be pleasant to be cut off in the prime of life, Mercy," croaked the withered old stick, solemnly shaking his head. "I wish you were a man instead of a woman, my love, just for an hour or two."

"What, so that I might go with you, do you mean?" Mercy asked.

"Yes. But there, you *are* a woman, and so it is no use talking, is it?"

"Of course it is. I meant to go with you from the first. It isn't often we put up the shutters so early, but we will this evening. Set about it at once, Tony, while I put my bonnet on."

It was a faint, a very faint, show of opposition that Anthony made to his sister's proposal; and just at the identical moment when Mr. Dyot was stealing away in the skiff of the jolly young waterman, the worthy pair set out for Rufford's Terrace.

They found (or rather Mr. Anthony found, for it was scarcely to be expected that a modest maiden lady such as Miss Gurd, would enter the common parlour of a tavern) Mr. Kettering still faithfully on guard. If the old gentleman was not perfectly sober—and what can a man who avails himself of the convenience of a drinking-room do but drink?—he was not the less vigilant.

"What news, sentinel?" inquired the doctor. There was nobody but the harness-maker in the parlour.

"An old woman came out, and the same old woman went in again, and a boy with a grocer's basket called, and a man that knocked with a double rap like a tax-collector; not a soul besides has passed in or out, I'll take an oath."

"That is all right then," remarked Mr. Gurd, rubbing his hands with a satisfied air. "I'll trouble you to wait here just a few minutes longer, and then I hope to bring you some news of your daughter, my friend."

"Is Mr. Dyot within?" asked the little doctor, as, with Mercy bringing up the rear, he knocked at the door of the house in Rufford's Terrace.

"Yes, sir," answered the old woman who responded. "What name, sir?"

"Never mind the name, we are old friends; we will go up."

And up they went, Mr. Gurd leading the way, and knocked at Mr. Dyot's door.

Nobody answered.

"He's out on the balcony, I suppose," whispered Anthony to his sister, and then he knocked again, louder this time.

No response.

Mr. Gurd gently tried the door; it was locked and the key was inside. Mr. Gurd knocked a sharp rat-tat with the knob of his umbrella against the panel, producing a noise loud enough to bring up the old woman from below.

"Perhaps he went out unknown to me, sir," she remarked.

"No; he is at home; he has turned the key on the inside," returned the doctor, "it is very strange that he does not hear the knocking;" and Anthony glanced nervously at his sister. What if he had goaded the poor gentleman to self-destruction, and he was now lying along the floor stark and beyond hearing? He knocked again louder than ever, and shook the door.

"Perhaps he is ill, sir; in a fit, may be," suggested the old lady, in a frightened voice. "He is a strange gentleman, to me, ma'am; I know nothing about him."

"If you think that he is ill, we can't do better than make our way in to him as speedily as possible. I am a medical man, and his friend."

And as though this was sufficient warrant for such a proceeding, the doctor applied his shoulder vigorously to the door, and it yielded suddenly.

Gone!

There was his chair at the table, on

which writing materials were strewn as though he had but just risen from work; there were his slippers, lying as though they had been hurriedly kicked off; there were a pair of boot-hooks, one on the floor, the other on a chair; and the close-fitting velvet cap he wore in-doors. There were the open window and the flapping window-curtain, and the broad expanse of black water, dotted with twinkling lamps that shone like glow-worms on a green meadow. There was the great black trunk that contained—with the great exception—the whole of Mr. Dyot's worldly goods; but what the little doctor sought so anxiously—taking the old woman's candle out of her hand with an absence of ceremony that would have astonished her was she not already astonished to the fullest extent of her capacity, prying in cupboards and recesses, and peeping under the bedstead even—he did not discover, and that was the black leather bag, the receptacle of the treasure.

"Oh dear! I didn't think that he was the kind of gentleman to hide under the bed or in a cupboard, or I certainly should have demanded a reference with him," exclaimed the old lady of the house, much alarmed at the doctor's strange behaviour and his muttered bad language and oaths when he failed to discover the object of his search. As for Mercy, she was so stupefied with rage and disappointment that her sarcastic safety-valve was choked, and worked but feebly.

"Why don't you look up the chimney, Tony? What's in that birdcage in the corner?"

But Tony took no heed. With a growl like that of a dog robbed of his meat, and forgetting that he still held the candle in his hand, he stepped out on to the balcony and gazed below, where the water was raising itself in little noisy leaps against the wall, and stared out before him, and to the left, and to the right. The brisk air blew the candle out, which was well for the old lady of the house, considering her nervous condition; for the face with which Master Anthony presently brought in from the balcony was not the prettiest in its expression.

"Good gracious, sir! You don't suspect that the gentleman has drowned himself, do you?" the old lady inquired.

"I wish to the Lord that he [here Mercy plucked him by the coat-tail]—that he had told me that he should be away from home this evening; it would have saved us a long journey and a pound in coach-hire. However, it can't be helped. I will come again to-morrow."

"Then you think that he has merely gone out, sir?"

"To be sure; what else? Come along, my dear, there is no use in staying here any longer."

"But the door, sir? How came it locked on the inside?"

"Well, it's quite clear that it was *not* locked inside. It was my mistake. Tell him, if you please, when he returns that I [Mr. Wiggings] will call on him in the morning."

Mr. Wiggings's knees trembled so that it was a miracle how he contrived to take such long strides down the stairs. When the outer door closed on the disappointed pair, Mercy was about to set her safety-valve in operation again, when, catching sight, by the light of the overhanging lamp, of her brother's madly-furious face, she charitably refrained. Opportunely, as such things at times happen, an empty hackney-coach passed at that moment, the driver waving his whip in sign that he wanted a job. Mr. Gurd beckoned him.

"Where to, sir?"

"Close by the Monument, London Bridge."

Just as the coach started a man's voice was heard calling, "Hi! Stop a minute!" On which the driver pulled up.

It was old Mr. Kettering. Dreading the possibility that the news Dr. Gurd had promised to bring him presently concerning his Mary might be bad news, he had hurried to fortify himself with sundry further libations of brandy, hot and strong; and the face that he put in at the coach-window was scarcely that of a teetotaller.

"What, going off like that? Did you forget me? Make room, and let me come in."

"Be off!" cried out Anthony, snapping out the words with a ferocity that compelled Mr. Kettering to draw back.

"But my daughter, sir! You promised

to bring me some news of my poor gal, and ——"

"D—n your poor gal and the whole confounded crew of you!" interrupted the furious little doctor. "Drive on, coachman!"

So the coachman drove on, leaving the old harness-maker a spectacle to behold as he stood, gasping and gesticulating, in the middle of the road.

Mr. Gurd was the first to break the painful silence.

"Phew! What will be the end of it?" he exclaimed, more to himself than his sister.

Mercy had it at her tongue's tip to reply, "Jewels and gems; diamonds fit for a queen to wear!" but, by an effort, she resisted the temptation, and in lieu tendered him a little comfort.

"You were lucky to get that fifty pounds at all events."

"Pooh! Fifty pounds! Just the price that the scamp's address cost me," replied her brother, reckless of the consequences of imparting such a terrible item of news in a manner so sudden.

"You never mean to say that," gasped Mercy.

"Gave a cheque for fifty to the thief that I shot. Obliged to do it; couldn't get rid of him without? What odds? We may as well go to the devil with a hop, skip, and a jump as creep there." And Mr. Gurd, with the recklessness of despair, pulled his hat over his eyes and leant back in the corner with his arms folded. It was quite as well for his peace that he did administer the staggerer conveyed in the information to his sister concerning the fifty pounds' cheque. The weight of it immediately plunged her down to the lowest depths of grief, and, sinking back to her corner of the coach, she abandoned herself to tears, the silent flow of which was only interrupted by frequent gasps and sobs.

Not another word was said until the vehicle arrived at Old Fish Street, and the driver dismounted to let out his passengers.

"Shall I knock, sir?" said he.

He asked the question just as Anthony was stepping out, but instead of replying that worthy shrank back again, clutching his sister's shoulder with a trembling hand.

"There is a light, Mercy; a light!" he whispered, in a frightened voice.

"A light! Where?"

"In the kitchen; I saw it shining up through the grating."

"Why! who can it be?"

"Who? Who *can* it be but one person?"

"But she couldn't get out; how could she? What does she do waiting down there if she has got out?"

"Shall I knock at the door, mister?" again asked the coachman.

"No, thank you; we have a key," replied the doctor. "That will do; good-night!"

"We must go in and—and face it, I suppose," Anthony observed, his teeth chattering. "Shall I go first, Mercy?"

"No; let me go first. Perhaps she has gone. That's it, you may depend," said Mercy, with a sigh of relief. "She has got out, and gone and left the light burning."

"Ay! I never thought of that. Come along!"

But at that instant there appeared on the window-blind the shadow of some person within. The shadow not of a woman, but of a man, with a pipe in his mouth and smoke issuing therefrom. Whoever it was he seemed to have just now arrived at the fact that a coach had stopped at the door, and he came to the window, and, putting the blind a little aside, looked up. This they saw him do, though they couldn't make out his face.

"Who on earth can it be?" whispered Anthony, quaking.

"We had best wait here until a constable passes, and get him to go in with us," said Mercy, little less alarmed than her brother.

But as they spoke the door was opened with a suddenness that caused the doctor to utter a cry and take a backward jump off the step.

"Don't be alarmed. I thought your lodger, Mr. Tomkins, you know, might take the liberty of letting himself in and blowing a cloud in the kitchen till you came home. Come along; my brother Micah's downstairs."

It was Master Blake.

CHAPTER XVI.

IN WHICH THE MESSRS. BLAKE UNDERTAKE A JAIL DELIVERY.

BRUISED and battered as he was, with his dandified clothes disarranged, his shoulder bandaging displaced, and his wound bleeding afresh, thankful was Mr. Blake to discover that his ignominious flight from the harness-maker's shop was not disputed. "I'm well out of *that* mess," said he, as, bolting up Church Street, he so made his way to Notting Hill, where there was a coach-stand. "If I meddle again in this precious business I deserve to be nicked, that's all. By the Lord Harry! what a narrow shave!" and so straightening his attire a bit, and recovering his serenity as he walked in the shadow of the trees that skirted the road, he presently hailed a coach and rode home to Spitalfields, stopping only for a moment on his way to the banking-house on which Mr. Gurd's cheque was made payable, and obtaining the cash without demur.

But although, as he had most justly observed, he was well out of the mess, he could not rest contented with matters as they stood. He was ashamed equally of his failure, and of the hoax that had been put on him, and which had been the cause of it. He bought his young woman a pair of earrings—a present he had long promised her the first time he had a lucky windfall. They were splendid ornaments, with imitation diamonds and rubies of prodigious size. She was passionately attached to the robber, and would sooner have blistered her tongue than say a word hurtful to his feelings any day.

"Lor! how beautiful! and he's my own good boy for thinking of me," said she, as she kissed him for the gift. "What handsome stones! are they real, Ted?"

"Real be hanged," replied Blake, with a laugh. "D'ye think I've been looting a gold-mine, Poll?"

"Lor! now; not real, ain't they—only

coloured glass! Never mind; I am as proud of 'em, since you bought 'em, as though they was real and worth ever so much, ain't I, dear?" and she kissed him again, harder than before.

"Of course you are, Poll," said Mr. Blake; but he didn't think so. "They might have been real, if I hadn't been such a confounded jackass," he mused, as he turned from Poll and walked discontentedly down-stairs.

There he encountered Micah, who was downright savage; as it seemed to him, poor young man, he had reason to be.

"But you ain't going to let it drop like this?" remarked Micah.

"Certainly not. I'm just going to have a cup of tea and a wash, and then I'm off again to Old Fish Street, or else to Kensington. I'm not sure which; but I think that I prefer Gurd's as being the hottest," replied his brother, ironically.

But Micah affected to receive what his brother said as in earnest. Indeed, it bore so exactly on an idea that had suddenly ripened in his fertile brain that it is not impossible that he so regarded it.

"To be sure!" he exclaimed, brightening up; "that's the game, Teddy. I'll come with you. We'll take the old thief by storm."

Master Blake laughed to see how the joke was going.

"I'll come with you," pursued Micah. "If, as you say, we start as soon as you have had your tea, we shall probably get there—to Old Fish Street—in time to catch our gentleman just returned, and gloating over his share of the booty with his sister."

Blake pricked up his ears. New views were dawning on him.

"Don't you see," continued the cunning Micah, "it would be precious little use his coming the old soldier over you about the address unless he meant stealing a march? He sent you the wrong way while he went the right. While old Kettering was pummelling you amongst the straps and bradawls the old fox was not unlikely making his haul out of Mr. Dyot. Don't you see?"

Master Blake was much struck by his brother Micah's ingenuity. "I tell you what it is, Micah," said he, shaking that gentleman by the hand; "if you wasn't such a precious white-livered chap you'd be an ornament to the profession. It shall be as you propose; after tea we'll start."

Although dark, it was not very late in the evening when the brothers arrived at Old Fish Street; great, however, was their astonishment at finding the shutters of the pill-shop closed, and no light visible at any window.

"He has made the grand haul and bolted at once, you may depend," exclaimed the despairing Micah. "We are too late. I knew that we should be. Shouldn't wonder if his old cat of a sister met him at London Bridge, and the two have cut off in the German packet."

"And I shouldn't wonder if the two were, at this very moment, picking something nice for supper in the back parlour," remarked his more sanguine brother; "don't let us halloo before we're hurt;" and as he spoke he rang a brisk peal at the bell.

Nothing came of it, so he rang another, and still another, very much to the astonishment of the captive in the back attic;

who, through fifteen weary hours, had kept fasting vigil.

"Either they are out, or they won't open; if the latter, probably the door is bolted; let us see."

And, so saying, the burglar took from his pocket a small and handy tool or two which, as a professional man, he invariably carried with him, and applying them to the lock, the door yielded without the least resistance.

The interior gained, Mr. Blake struck a light, and then discovered, conveniently standing on a bracket in the passage, a candle and matches, which was conclusive evidence that the good folk of the house had gone out, designing to return not till after dark.

"So that they haven't gone to France or Germany either, Micah, my boy; and we are in good time after all," exclaimed Master Blake, clapping his brother on the shoulder, delightedly. "This is better and better. My eyes, Mic! fancy the agreeable surprise it will give the old shark when he comes home with the swag and I open the door to him!"

"But where's the gal, I wonder?" remarked Micah, who was equally pleased. "You said there was a gal, didn't you?"

"I've precious good reasons for knowing that there was a gal," returned Mr. Blake, wagging his head in grateful remembrance. "I should like you to have seen her, Micah. I could forgive her old tiger of a father ten times over, for the sake of the good turn she did me."

"Prettier than Poll, was she?"

"Poll!" Had the young lady alluded to heard the contemptuous emphasis with which her true love pronounced her name, she would scarcely have felt flattered. "No; not that sort at all, Mic; the reg'lar right kind of woman; not a toy. The sort of wench, you know, that——there, what's the good of my trying to describe her?"

"Are you spooney on her, Ted?" his brother asked, laughing.

"*Me!* It's likely, ain't it?" And Mr. Blake, as his brother perceived by the light of the tallow candle, looked curiously red in the face and sheepish. "She was started off this morning, I reckon," he continued; "after what she had seen, they must have been glad to get rid of her."

"And a good start too, if she had only left behind her directions where old Gurd keeps his liquor. I should like a nip of something comfortable, Teddy."

"Funking, are you?" suggested the other, blandly.

"Funking; no. But it is cold work standing here in the passage. You ought to know your way about a bit in this crib. Isn't there nowhere where we can sit down and make ourselves comfortable while we wait?"

"Come along o' me, and I'll show you my old lodgings, and the iron safe where bogie kept his bushels of diamonds before he ran away from his kind landlord," said the playful burglar. "First of all, though, Micah, put the bolt on the door; it will be safer."

And, Teddy leading the way up, they went to the room Mr. Dyot had lately occupied, and where Mr. Blake's wounds were dressed.

There were the disordered bed and the bedraggled bed clothes, with smirches of blood on the counterpane and on the pillow, which, viewed together with the empty strong-box, with its door swinging ajar, made the place appear as though a murder and robbery had been recently there committed. Micah shivered.

"If you haven't got anything more lively than this to show a fellow," said he, "I prefer going down into the passage again."

Now it happened at this identical moment that Mary, in the back garret overhead, after listening in tremendous anxiety, first to the strange ringing at the door-bell, and again to the sound of unknown footsteps ascending the stairs, thought fit to exercise her lungs in the shrillest of screams by way of attracting the attention of any person besides the Gurds who might happen to be in the house.

The door of her bed-chamber had warped away from its setting, leaving a space at top wide enough to thrust a finger through; and, standing on a chair and applying her mouth to this interstice, the peal that Mary caused to ring through the silent house might have disturbed consciences less guilty than those possessed by Mr. Micah and his brother. The former stared aghast, while his under jaw fell helplessly away from his upper.

"The infernal place is haunted!" he gasped, catching his brother by the sleeve, and holding on tight.

"It was a woman's voice," returned the more self-possessed Teddy.

"Very likely; somebody that the old villain has poisoned and buried in the cellar, I shouldn't wonder," said Micah, in a sweat of terror. "If we must wait, let us come and wait in the passage, not up here."

"Not I," replied Master Blake, a possibility of the true state of the case occurring to him; "we shall be nearer to the cellar, stupidhead, if we go down to the passage; I am going to try a flight higher."

And, so saying, he shook off the cowardly Micah; and, candle in hand, in six strides reached the topmost landing, where the padlocked door was, and the great bolt shot into the oaken doorpost.

"Anybody here?" he exclaimed, rapping at the door with his fist. "Didn't I hear a woman's voice?"

"For God's sake let me out, whoever you may be; I have been a prisoner here since early morning."

Harsh and dry as the voice was, Master Blake recognized it instantly. With a cry of amazement he at once drew the bolt, but the padlock was secure, and he had only one hand to work with.

"Come up here, Micah!" he cried hurriedly; and up Micah came, and finding that no more formidable task was before him than bursting a pad-lock, he achieved the job in a twinkling, and the captive was revealed.

Fifteen hours' incarceration had not at all improved Miss Kettering's personal appearance. Her eyes were red and swollen, her hair dishevelled, and her hands bruised and bleeding from her unavailing efforts to force the door or the window bars. She was famished for want of food, and so utterly exhausted that her unexpected deliverance occasioned her more emotion than her strength could support; and uttering but a few incoherent words of thanks, she turned deadly pale as she stepped out of her prison, and swooned then and there.

To be sure, any one would have thought that his brother Micah was right in his surmise that Master Edward was "spooney," at least, on the young woman, compared with whom the faithful Poll of Spitalfields seemed odious.

While Micah held her he hurried into the little bed-room and procured a chair and a pillow, so that her head might rest easy; and then he skipped down-stairs with the light, and was heard banging and slamming closet and cupboard doors, and in less than two minutes ascended again with eager strides, and made his appearance with Mr. Gurd's own particular brandy-bottle grasped by the neck, and which he had discovered in its hiding-place in the parlour in the rear of the shop.

"Where is he?" was the frightened question she first asked on recovering her senses.

"Who do you mean, miss?—the doctor, Mr. Gurd? He has gone out; so has his sister; they have gone together, I believe," Master Blake replied. "You know me, don't you, miss? I'm the man that——"

"Yes, yes; I know you," Mary interrupted, with a shudder, and turning her head away in a manner that was extremely hurtful to the sensitive robber's feelings. "Why are you here? Are you set to watch me while they are away? Are you my jailers?"

"It doesn't look much like it, miss," returned Master Blake, with mild reproach in his tone, as he pointed at the ruined fastenings of the door. "P'r'aps you'll excuse me asking why are *you* here, and who it was that shut you up in this da—— this cruel sort of manner? Was it Gurd? Don't mind telling us; we are friends, if you'll allow me to say as much—*your* friends, not his, understand me. We've come here to settle a score with him; and, if it is he who has played you this trick, your account may as well go down with ours, and he shall wipe it all off at once."

"I only want to get away," replied Mary; "if you can enable me to do that I shall indeed be grateful. Pray let me go away from this dreadful house."

"There are the stairs and the street beyond. You are free to go," returned Mr. Blake. "Only, before you do go, just answer me a question, like a brave girl as you are. Does this Gurd know where to find Mr. Dyot?"

"I am afraid so," Mary replied, after a moment's hesitation.

"Did you tell him? I heard you say that you knew—that you had his address, and could find your way to him in half an hour."

"I do know, and I believe that he knows. He went up to my room in the night and stole the address I mentioned out of my box. He stole that and something else a thousand times more precious." And, at the bitter recollection, Mary's white face flushed red with scorn and indignation.

"What else was it that he robbed you of?" asked the thief, eagerly. "Was it money? What was it? Tell me, and he shall return it to you if it is worth five hundred pounds. He shall, by G—d!"

"It was not of the value of a pin to anyone but myself," returned Mary, further exciting Mr. Blake's tender compassion by beginning to cry. "It was cowardly to rob me of it."

"Lord send you would tell what it was," said the chivalrous burglar. "D'ye think it's in the house now? It wouldn't take me ten minutes to overhaul every box and drawer the crib contains."

But, for reasons that are obvious, Mary declined the suggestion.

"It would be useless to look for it or to ask him about it," said she; "it is lost to me beyond recovery. May I go now? Pray don't detain me."

"If she's going she'd best go at once," suggested Micah. "They may be back any moment."

He began to be afraid that spooney concernfor the young woman's affairs might spoil his brother for the real business in hand.

"Just one more question," remarked Mr. Blake. "You can't deny that I've done you a good turn. You did me one, and I haven't forgot it; I shall never forget it. The one I ask of you now is quite a little 'un compared with it. Where *has* Mr. Dyot gone to live?"

"I just now told you that I have been robbed of the direction he gave me," Mary evasively answered.

"And you don't recollect from reading it?"

"I don't recollect." Which was a fib.

"Well I won't press you. You're a staunch wench, and if you don't have good luck, you'll get less than your deservings." And, accompanying Mary down the stairs, he unbolted the door.

"This is a rum meeting and parting, isn't it, miss?" he remarked, with an odd sort of look, and one that sat uncomfortably on his brazen visage. "D'ye mind shaking hands?"

It wasn't much to ask.

CHAPTER XVII.

MR. GURD COMES TO TERMS WITH HIS UNWELCOME GUESTS; AND MASTER EDWARD BLAKE BECOMES THE CUSTODIAN OF MARY KETTERING'S PRECIOUS RELIC.

"WHAT do you say to coming down into the kitchen and having a glass and a pipe till our landlord returns?" suggested Master Blake, as he rejoined Micah, who was in the highest degree disgusted at his brother's behaviour.

So they carried the brandy-bottle down into the kitchen, and there made themselves as comfortable as circumstances would permit. There they were when Mr. Gurd and his sister, returned from their disappointing journey to Rufford's Terrace, arrived home in a coach.

"Come in; glad to see you both; Micah's down-stairs," exclaimed Master Edward

Blake, as he opened the door to them, at the same time politely putting out a saving hand to Miss Mercy, who, in her fright, was staggering backward off the top step.

Mr. Gurd's first idea was to shoot the burglar dead where he stood, and to that end his hand stole round towards the armed coat-tail pocket; but, checking the murderous inclination, he hastily stepped off the pavement, and it was on his tongue tip to halloa "Police!" at the top of his voice; but timely reflection arrested this design also. What if the constables came, and, searching the house, discovered the padlocked prison? Anyhow, it would be better to ascertain what had occasioned the ruffians to favour him with the visit, and what they expected to gain by it. He walked into the passage, taking his sister with him, and closed the door.

"What does this outrage mean?" he indignantly demanded.

"Don't call it an outrage; it is merely a friendly call, partner," responded Master Blake with a grin. "What an ungrateful fellow you are! We prepare what we think will be a pleasant surprise for you, and this is the return!"

"How long have you been here?" the doctor asked.

"How long? Oh, a precious long while! We've found enough to amuse us, though, roaming about the house."

"*Have* you been roaming over the house?" Gurd exclaimed, in a voice quivering with rage and terror.

"We have been taking that liberty, Micah and I," returned Master Blake, rubbing his hands, courteously.

"Well, and what did you discover, you scoundrelly breaker of honest men's houses?" demanded the little doctor, his hand once again wandering to the region of his coat-tail; "did you find anything that paid you for your search?"

"Thank you, we did [Mr. Gurd compressed his lips nervously, in apprehension of what was coming next]; we discovered a bottle of excellent brandy [Mr. Gurd's lips parted, and he breathed freely]. We were remarking on its fine flavour when you arrived in your carriage. There's a drop left, and you must be chilly after your journey, which I hope was to your satisfaction. Come down-stairs and make yourselves happy."

Mr. Anthony was puzzled as to the course that, under the very peculiar circumstances, should be adopted. He looked askance at his sister.

"Let us have no more of this, brother Anthony," said she, meeting Master Blake's impudent gaze defiantly; "it is evident, sir [this to Teddy], that you are mistaken in the sort of people you have to deal with. If my brother, ignorant of your true character, has been betrayed into certain dealings with you, and has been compelled to pay monstrous sums for your services, that is no reason why we should still suffer from your persecution."

"Ay, you villain; how dare you break into the house of a respectable tradesman?" exclaimed Anthony, taking the cue; "take yourself off instantly, you and your precious brother, or I'll raise the neighbourhood. I'm in earnest; by ——, I am," continued the little doctor, glaring savagely, and stamping with his mite of a foot. "I know what you know, and I don't care that for you; say as you like, do as you like; go and be hanged. The game has taken a turn that you don't expect."

These last words were rather screamed than said by the wrathful doctor, so that Micah, wondering what the row was about, came up the kitchen stairs without his hat, and smoking a short pipe—presenting a spectacle scarcely likely to soothe Mr. Gurd's extreme exasperation. The words last uttered by that gentleman, however, so far from daunting the first robber, appeared rather to reassure him.

"There you are mistaken, partner," returned he, coolly, as he audaciously stooped to re-light his cigar at the candle Miss Mercy held in her trembling hand. "I know all about the turn the game has taken; Micah put me up to it. It is that that brings us here. Don't make a fool of yourself, my little man. It's very unpleasant for you and your amiable sister, no doubt, but it can't be helped. We've only come for our dues, and our dues we mean to have. It was not a bad trick you put on me this morning. Many a fellow would have held a grudge against you for it; I don't. It was a chance that you couldn't afford to throw away."

"What trick do you mean?" inquired Mr. Gurd. "The trick of being fool enough to be bullied out of fifty pounds?"

"No; not that trick; the other one, my clever partner; the palming the *wrong* address on me while you made good use of the *right* one."

"And what do you imagine is the good use I have made of the right address?" And Anthony grinned maliciously.

"You are an idiot to hold conversation with such ruffians," interposed his sister, the gall of her nature cruelly disturbed by this allusion to the fruitlessness of the mission to Rufford's Terrace.

"No, I am not," returned Anthony. "I have told him that I don't care a rap, a single button-shank, for him or that other skulking thief, and I don't mind convincing him *why* I don't. Now, Mr. Housebreaker, what use do you suppose I have made of Mr. Dyot's address?"

"I will tell you. You have paid the unlucky beggar a visit, you have bullied and frightened him out of a share of the booty he bolted with from here, and now you've come home with it, and are naturally a little out of temper to find a couple of friends waiting to welcome you and cry shares."

Mr. Gurd laughed a laugh that was undoubtedly genuine.

"Now, look you what a foolish thing it is to jump at conclusions," he exclaimed. "It is quite true that I hoaxed you this morning about the address; it is equally true that I did so with a view to making the best of the preposterous bargain you insisted on; but what is *not* true is, that I am a gainer. I am the poorer, for I am the coach hire out of pocket. He has gone —took fright and fled. Where, I don't know; and I shan't inquire. Perhaps he is now lying at the bottom of the river with his infernal treasure slung round his neck as they attach a brick to drown a mangey dog. Wherever he is, d—n him; I've done with him. Here's his late address—make the most of it. I give you ten minutes to clear out of my house. If you are not gone by that time I'll have the constables here. Come up-stairs, Mercy. There's nothing down here they can steal but the tables and chairs."

"We shan't take the pills, you may depend," remarked the facetious Micah, calling up the stairs after the retreating forms of the brother and sister.

"Now, what's the next move?" Micah inquired. "It's all lies about Dyot bolting, of course?"

"No; it's all true about Dyot bolting; that's the worst of it," returned his brother. "The devil himself couldn't lie like that."

"D'ye think that he means what he says about the constables?"

"To be sure he does. No fear of that," returned his brother, coolly.

"Well, then, don't you think that we can't do better than ——"

"Be off? I should think so if there wasn't another card to play. He means all that he says now; but he'll find out something that may make him alter his tune presently. Hark! I thought so. He *has* found it."

So he had. Leaving his sister for a moment in the sitting-room, he stole up to the attic—and, of course, made the unwelcome discovery. Down he came to Mercy in a fright.

"She's gone!" he exclaimed; "they've let her out, and she has gone;" and then, quite distracted by this continued heaping up of misfortune, without awaiting any observation the startling information might elicit from his sister, he hurried down the stairs to the kitchen, to which Mr. Blake and his brother, hearing him coming, had promptly retreated, and were now sitting at the table, smoking and drinking quite at their ease.

"Where is the girl? What have you done with her?" he cried, confronting Mr. Blake.

Now, here it may be remarked, that ever since the time when Mary Kettering, actuated by simple motives, interfered for the burglar's safety, Mr. Gurd had not been without certain vague suspicions that there was some sort of understanding between the parties. The thought struck him at the time, and was strengthened by the burglar's eager defence of the young woman when, as the reader may recollect, he was closely questioned by the doctor on the occasion of his bragging of his "friend in court." Perhaps *that* is the true cause of his stealing into my house to-night! was the idea that now suddenly flitted into the doctor's bewildered mind. "There is some kind of compact between them, and, being unable to meet with her to-day, he suspected something wrong, and came here to see about it."

"Where is the girl?" he exclaimed. "What have you done with her?"

It would have been clear to the merest dunce that Mr. Gurd was in terror lest the burglars had "done something with her," and Mr. Blake was shrewd man of business enough to be aware that the doctor's terror was his opportunity; therefore he answered,

"The girl! Oh! she's all right, old gentleman. Don't you trouble yourself about the girl; I'll look after her."

Whereupon Mr. Anthony rashly proceeded further to expose his weak point to the enemy.

"You ruffian!" said he; "you have been in league with her all along. You know where she is now; I'd bet a thousand pounds that you do."

"To be sure I do; I never said that I didn't, did I?" returned Mr. Blake, helping himself to brandy and water. "I've packed her off to a friend of mine. I don't blame you for shutting her up, considering what she could do for you if she chose to open her mouth; but, hang it, Gurd, you might have given her a bit of food. She's awfully fierce against you, I can tell you—much as ever I could do to get her to be off before you came home. You'll have to stump up handsome, if you want her to keep her tongue quiet."

"Not another rap—not so much as a single farthing," Mr. Gurd responded, wagging his head, determinedly.

"Oh dear, yes! In the first place, you know you must restore to her that other little matter that, besides Dyot's address, you stole from her."

"Stole from her?"

"Took from her—got out of her. I've no wish to hurt your feelings."

The letter with the little black curl in it had quite slipped out of Mr. Gurd's memory. He thought, to be sure, that, as her accomplice, she had informed Master Blake concerning the sum she had deposited with her employers as a guarantee for her honesty, and was relieved at the prospect of getting off so easily.

"That's good, too, to speak of a thing as stolen that is placed voluntarily in a man's hand," said the doctor. "The twenty pounds is hers, and of course she shall have it."

"Of course she shall," returned Blake, evincing not the least astonishment; "she told me to be sure that I didn't come away without it. Perhaps you'd better hand it over while you think of it."

"Suppose I hold it over for a month or so, and then give it her on condition that she doesn't go talking about me or my affairs?"

"About that affair that she hinted of before me, amongst the rest, eh?—that little affair that might lead to your taking a airing up Newgate Hill one fine Monday morning?"

This was a random shot, but it told, making the miserable doctor writhe again.

"Tattling of my affairs generally, I mean," said he; "if she refrains from doing so for a month, there are her twenty pounds."

"Twenty pounds, indeed!" Mr. Blake observed, contemptuously; "why, you'd be glad to pay down twenty twenties rather than she should go to a justice and peach all that she knows of you and your sister."

"All she knows of you and your sister!" Mr. Gurd's guilty conscience immediately provided a billet for this second random bullet let fly by the wily burglar. Clearly it was an allusion to Mercy's *private* business, a clue to which the young woman might possibly have discovered. Possibly! At that identical instant the discovery of Mrs. Craven's letter in the young woman's clothes-box flashed to his mind, and then the whole business became clear enough.

"I wish I were ten thousand miles away from here. I wish my fingers had been burnt off before I was tempted to meddle with this confounded business," he ejaculated, looking helplessly from one scoundrel to the other.

"Well, why don't you go ten thousand miles away? Who hinders you? All that you have got to do is to make matters comfortable all round, and you may sail in the very first ship that happens to be travelling so far as you would like to go," said Mr. Blake, magnanimously.

"Or perhaps you would not object to see *us* ten thousand miles away?" put in Micah; "that would suit you quite as well, I should say. We did think of emigrating, didn't we, Teddy?"

"What do you mean when you say 'we'?" Mr. Gurd asked, after a pause.

"All parties concerned," returned Micah.

"Mary and me, and Micah," said Master Blake.

"But you would'nt go! You would fleece me again, and you wouldn't go after all. Who can believe such rascals?" whined poor Mr. Gurd, in dire distress.

"Hand over our share of the booty and see, before you begin to cry out," observed Master Blake.

"I repeat to you that I have no booty," returned Mr. Anthony, striking the table passionately. "May I drop dead where I stand if I have touched a penny of booty or a penny's worth!"

"All the worse for you," replied the merciless Master Blake; "all the worse for you, if it is true; but I don't believe it. You whine about your injuries; damme, look at mine! Time wasted; made a tool and a fool of; shot at with deliberate intent to murder; jeered at as a muff amongst my friends. Is all that nothing?"

"Well, well; it is a most unfortunate business, and I suppose that you really do think that you have a grievance against me, young man," said Mr. Gurd, in a conciliatory tone, and feeling convinced of how useless it was to debate the matter with a couple of such thoroughpaced rogues. "If you don't believe me in what I have told you as to my disappointment at Stangate, I can't help it. But it is quite true; and all I want now is to wash my hands of the ugly business. I am only a poor man, but I am willing to make a sacrifice for my indiscretion. What little sum now, will you take to go away and never come back here again?"

"No little sum," returned Mr. Blake, promptly.

"Will you take another twenty pounds in addition to the twenty that belongs to the girl?"

"Let us see!" returned Mr. Blake, using his fingers to assist him in his calculation. "There are three of us; threes in twenty, six and two over. Threes in two pounds, thirteen and one over. That would be six pounds thirteen and fourpence a head! Couldn't you spring the other eightpence and make it even money, good Mr. Gurd?"

"I'll double it, and I won't say another penny," Mr. Gurd said, after a few moments of painful consideration.

"Double the forty?"

"No. Double the twenty—sixty altogether, that is—and you shall give me an acknowledgment stating that the story of the attempted burglary and the rescue of the young woman from the attic is all a gross fabrication for the purpose of extorting money, and that you humbly pray my forgiveness. You must all three sign it."

"Then that knocks the scheme on the head at once," returned Master Blake. "I'll no more think of laying such a document before my Polly to sign than I would think of eating it. You must leave her to me. If I say that I'll prevent her troubling you, I'll do it."

"That's the same thing. You two will sign it. It's a mere matter of form, of course."

"Sixty pounds; and that little something that you took, along with Dyot's address, out of my young woman's clothes-box. You know what I mean."

"What, the letter and the bit of baby's hair? If it's in existence you shall have it; it's of no use to us. I'll go and make inquiry." And away he went.

What transpired between him and his sister cannot be told, for the door was close shut, and they conversed in whispers. There is little more to tell of what meanwhile transpired between the two rogues in the kitchen; for, as soon as Mr. Gurd's back was turned, Master Edward Blake exclaimed,

"The letter and the bit of baby's hair!

What does *that* mean?" And Micah having addressed to him two or three remarks and received no answer, turned sulky and said no more.

In ten minutes Mr. Gurd returned, carrying the agreement ready drawn up for signing, and a crumpled letter.

"It is all right," said he, in reference to the latter; "it was a wonder that the bit of hair was not lost, for it slipped out into my sister's pocket. It's safe inside now, however, and here's a cheque for the sixty pounds, and here's a pen ready dipped in ink."

Master Blake received the crumpled letter, then signed the confession, and then took the cheque; but he said not one word until he reached the street, and then he merely repeated his previous observation,

"A letter and a bit of baby's hair; now what can *that* mean?" and immediately relapsed into his previous moody silence.

CHAPTER XVIII.

IN WHICH MARY KETTERING FINDS MORE SATISFACTION THAN IN ANY THAT PRECEDES IT.

It was not a pleasant night, that on which, by the interference of the Messrs. Blake, Mary was released from her prison, inasmuch there was falling a thick, drizzling rain, and the way was miry, and the church clocks were chiming eleven as mire splashed and with her clothes saturated she reached Stangate, and, inquiring of a watchman, was directed to Rufford's Terrace. There was a lamp burning at the house the man pointed out as No. 3, and, as Mary thankingly perceived in the distance, another light was burning in an upper chamber. So, with a palpitating heart, she hurried forward, wondering as to her reception and the news she should presently hear, and ascended the house steps; but there she encountered a check that caused her to hesitate before she touched the bell. On the threshold of the door there sat a man with his hat thrown back, revealing his grey hairs. He sat like a tipsy man, with his arms on his knees and his face on his arms. As Mary's dress rustled against the railings, he suddenly raised his head, and, after regarding her for a moment, uttered a startled cry of affright, and sprang to his feet. Mary Kettering recognized him instantly.

"Father!"

"What! you, Polly! It's all true, then. You are what they made you out to be! At this time o' night, and blown about and bedraggled, like the commonest of 'em. Oh, God A'mighty! look at her!"

And truly, from the old harness-maker's misguided point of view, appearances were terribly against his daughter. It was now within an hour of midnight, and here she was at the door of the man who had been accused of betraying her to paths of vice and immorality. When her father said, "Look at her!" he himself did not do so; with a vast groan that seemed to shake his sturdy frame, he sank his head again, and still lower, on to his knees, and so remained. How he came seated on the steps of Mr. Dyot's lodgings is the easiest thing in the world to explain. When the reader last saw the bereaved old fellow he was standing in the roadway, amazed and quite taken aback by Dr. Gurd's extraordinary behaviour and his no less extraordinary reply to the harness-maker's interrogatory as to his lost daughter. "I'm not to be humbugged by a set of shuffling scoundrels in this way!" he exclaimed, in a fury, as Mr. Gurd drove off in his coach; and then, dashing across the road, he commenced such a hammering at the door of No. 3 as brought up the old lady fast as her trembling knees would allow, the foremost thought in her mind being that her late lodger had really committed suicide by jumping from his window, and that somebody had recovered his dead body and had brought it home. It was quite a relief to her to discover but one individual when she opened the door.

"I want to see Mr. Dyot," exclaimed old Kettering, abruptly.

"Bother Mr. Dyot; he'll be the death

of me, I think," returned she, in a pet. "He's gone out. He'll get warning to go, and never come back again, as soon as he returns."

"Are you sure, ma'am, that he's out? He didn't tell you to deny me?"

"Goodness bless the man, no. Perhaps you'd like to go up and pry and peep into all the cupboards for him, as the people that came inquiring just now did. He's not at home, I tell you; and he left no message with me for anybody."

"Will it be long before he returns, can you tell me?"

"I know nothing at all about it, my good man."

"Very good, then, I shall wait; if it's till five o'clock to-morrow morning, I shall wait;" and, as the old lady closed the door, down he sat on the threshold, where his daughter found him.

Poor Mary was terribly distressed. Be it remembered that, since that memorable day when she stole out of her father's house to take service at the abode of Mr. Gurd, she had neither seen nor heard from her parents, and was altogether unaware of the circumstances that had led to Mr. Kettering's acquaintance with the doctor, or of any of the events that had subsequently occurred.

"Speak to me, father," said she, laying her trembling hands on the old man's bowed head; "tell me how you came here, and why."

"Tell me how *you* came here, and why," echoed her father, looking up at her with his fishy old eyes, wet with tears. "Who is it that you expected to meet coming to this house?"

"Surely you cannot know the gentleman, father," Mary answered, quite innocently. "I came here to see a person named Dyot."

"What! you confess this to me? to your own father!" he exclaimed, starting up and regarding his daughter in blank amazement. "Do you dare to brag of your shame, and to me?"

And now, for the first time, Mary observed the black crape about the old man's hat.

"Father, how is mother?" she eagerly asked: "is she well?"

"Dead, thank heaven! Aren't you glad? You ought to be." And the old man spoke in a tone so cold and bitter that added more than can be told to the crushing weight of the doleful news.

"Dead!—mother dead!" And, to save herself from falling, Mary caught at his arm and there held on.

"Ay, to be sure!" returned he, cruelly, as before. "What sort of a woman was your mother in your opinion that you are surprised that she should sink under the weight of infamy you cast on her? I am made of tougher stuff, worse luck, or I should have been spared this meeting. You had better sit down here by the side o' me. I, too, have come to see this Mr. Dyot; he is away from home it seems; we will wait for him and see him together."

"You have come to see him? What do you know of him? Why do you wish to see him? Who told you where he was to be found?"

"Your master, whose house you robbed and fled from in the night. Don't start away from me. I know all about it, you see. I may tell you, however, if it will bring you comfort, and if you have not already been made aware of it, that your friend, the scoundrel you came here to visit has been so generous as to recompense Mr. Gurd for his loss. I was this morning witness to his paying over the sum of one hundred pounds as a means of hushing up the pretty business. So you may sit down beside me, Mary, without fear of the constables—as far as I know—that is, as far as I know."

For several moments Mary sat quite silent, stunned and bewildered by the astounding words her father had uttered. Her mother dead; she accused of being a thief, or worse; Mr. Dyot paying a hundred pounds to screen her from the consequences of a robbery she had committed on Mr. Gurd; her father's acquaintance with Mr. Dyot, as well as with the doctor—it was a maze with a vengeance.

"Father," said she, at length, "who was it told you that Mr. Dyot was a scoundrel?"

The old fellow laughed bitterly. "Ay, stick up for him; it's the way with your sex, even the worst of 'em; besides it's his due, since he's been so kind to you. It was your master, who not only told me but showed me the true colour of your dear friend."

"And who was it that informed you that I—I was a thief?"

"Mr. Gurd. Who was better able to give me the information?"

"And that I had fled from his house in the night?"

"He told me that, too; and so you did. Did you not? You didn't deny it just now."

"And did you believe it, father? Do you believe all this?"

"I *know* that it is in part true; why not entirely so?" returned her father, severely. "I know from finding you here that the worst part of what has been told me is true. A thief is not the worst that a woman can be, Mary."

"Look at me, father," said Mary, lifting up his unwilling face with both hands. "Mother is dead, you tell me. Did she leave a message for me before she died?"

"Pshaw! what do you care about your

mother or her message? She died as she lived—a good, forgiving soul, and a woman worthy of a better daughter."

"But *did* she charge you with a message for me, father?"

"She said something about meeting you hereafter, in heaven. There's a likelihood of that, if things don't alter!"

"Listen to me, father; nay, don't turn your face away. Look at me and judge if I am speaking truth. If my mother's last wish, her last prayer, was that we might meet hereafter, I tell you that I hope it will be unheard and disregarded if there is one word of truth in the cruel accusations you bring against me."

"Why, how can that be?" exclaimed the old harness-maker, incredulously, though not without hope in his eyes. "That can hardly be made out, Mary. Didn't you just now confess that you have come here to-night to see this fellow?"

"I did so because it was my duty. I came to warn him against his enemies," Mary replied.

"And was it necessary to delay your visit till this hour?"

"I came here as soon as it was possible. Two hours since I was a prisoner——"

"A prisoner? and that is my innocent girl!" interrupted Kettering, his new-born hopes flickering low.

"A prisoner in the house of Doctor Gurd," continued Mary.

"What? A prisoner in the apothecary's own house till within the last two hours? Impossible! I myself was there this morning, in the shop, talking of you with him and his sister."

"And I was shut up in the attic, trapped there, and bolted and barred in. You have been deceived, father. This Doctor Gurd is a bad man: I believe that he would not stick at murder to ensure his wicked designs —I am sure that he would not."

"And this is quite true, Polly?" exclaimed Kettering, after a pause, and taking his daughter's cold hands in his own, which were very hot; "there is no truth at *all* in what I have been told, none *whatever.*"

"None whatever, if you have informed me of all that you were told."

"You did not take the jewels—in a drawer in the back parlour he said they were? Mary, you did not take his property? You did not steal off in the night?"

"Take me to him, and judge for yourself how innocent or guilty I am," returned Mary, quietly. "Take me somewhere, father; I feel cold and ill; I feel as though I should faint."

"Will you go home with me, Mary?" the old man asked, eagerly. "There is your little room just as you left it. It is quite too late to see into the rights and wrongs of this business to-night. It shall be seen to to-morrow, however; by the Lord Harry, it shall! Shall I get a coach and take you back with me to Kensington, Polly?"

And the coach was procured, and the coachman informed where he was to drive to. It is a long ride from Westminster to Kensington, but the strange story that Mary had to tell out-lasted it; so that by the time the familiar little shop was reached, she had still something left to tell.

"We're in a sad muddle, lass," said the old fellow, as they entered the old parlour, and the light that he struck discovered his eyes red with crying; "the loss of any woman four-and-thirty years his helpmate, is a blow to shake a man; but a woman such as she was, Polly!" And here the old gentleman broke down again, and his tears flowed as fresh as though this, their cause, had been discovered but yesterday. "Never mind; I'm not quite so bad off as I thought I was, thank the Lord! I've found my gal again; and it'll make a new man of me. But there's one thing you haven't told me, Polly—why did you go away from us; what was to be gained by it, my dear?"

They had walked up-stairs together and into the bed-room where the white dimity was hanging, and where Mary was born, and where her mother died; and there she told her father why she had gone away, what she went to seek, and what she had found, and what she had lost again so soon after finding it. Never in her life had she talked with him so freely before; nor would she now if he had not shown himself such a tender-hearted, tearful old stupid. His exhibitions of rage and indignation at certain parts of her narration, his outbursts of grief at others, his threats of vengeance against the Gurds, and his reiterated expressions of regret for his behaviour towards unfortunate Mr. Dyot, need not be here repeated; indeed, with the reader's permission, the father and daughter shall be left engaged at the blessed task of reconciliation, and the chapter be brought to an end.

CHAPTER XIX.

MR. MICAH GOES TO WORK "ON HIS OWN HOOK," BUT, AS FAR AS AT PRESENT APPEARS, DOES NOT CATCH MANY FISH.

As has been already intimated, Micah Blake was not over well satisfied with the manner in which his brother Teddy had conducted the Dyot business. He felt ill-used. To be sure, Teddy had behaved not unhandsomely in the way of division of spoil; but the spoil was so scanty. Counting up his share of it, he found that it amounted to very little more than twenty pounds, and, by the time he had bought himself some necessary clothing and disbursed a pound or two in defraying outstanding debts, he found the insignificant sum of five pounds remaining; and, to show his despising of it, he set to work, and in less than a week drank, and smoked, and squandered it away until it was melted down to a pound. Then, as a natural consequence, the brothers quarrelled, Edward flatly declining to meddle again in what was known between them as the "D" affair, and Micah declaring his intention to pursue the business single-handed.

A day or two after the quarrel, Micah made his appearance at Rufford's Terrace, guided thereto by the address which, as the reader is already aware, he possessed himself of when Mr. Gurd threw it down as now a drug in the market. There was a bill in the window of No. 3, announcing an apartment to let; and, observing it, Mr. Micah, having deliberated on the course he should pursue, marched boldly up the steps (he was decently dressed), and made inquiries as to lodgings.

"It is a very pleasant room, overlooking the river," said the old lady.

"Have you any other lodger, ma'am?" Micah blandly asked.

"No other lodger."

"May I be permitted to see the room?"

"To be sure, sir; but I must first ask you a question—can you give me respectable references?"

"For a thousand pounds, my dear ma'am, if necessary," returned the rogue, who, to do him justice, could act his part to perfection when he undertook a case in his own peculiar line. "You will not take it amiss if I require a similar favour in return, I am sure."

"Where may you be living at present, and how long have you lived there, sir?"

"If you will address your inquiries to Bullion and Walmsley, Turkey merchants, Lombard Street, I have no doubt that they will be answered in a satisfactory manner, ma'am;" and Mr. Micah, withdrawing his bandana from his pocket with a flourish, blew the blast of a wealthy man upon it.

"Thank you, sir!" returned the weak-minded old lady, curtseying, and not a little awed by the airs assumed by the member of the firm of Bullion and Walmsley, of Lombard Street. "You will excuse me, I'm sure; but you know, sir, there are so many bad characters that get themselves up to look like gentlemen, that one hardly knows the good from the bad, to judge from appearances. This way, sir."

The first thing that attracted Micah's attention as he entered the pleasant room overlooking the river, was the large black chest, the property of Mr. Dyot. He knew it well enough: he had helped carry it upstairs at Tadger's. He was not a little alarmed.

"I understood that the room was—was unoccupied, and awaiting a tenant, ma'am," said he.

"And so it is, sir. What has made you think otherwise?"

"That—those slippers and the smoking-cap, ma'am; they look as though they had been worn but just now. They are not part of the room's ordinary furniture, I presume?"

"They belong to the gentleman—or, rather, the person—that lately lodged here. I say 'person,' sir, because it is hard to believe any gentleman would have acted so."

"Ran away in your debt, eh? Quite your own fault, madam; you should be paid in advance—a month, three months; what does it matter to a lodger who is a gentleman? It is my invariable practice to pay so, I assure you."

"Oh, no, sir; he did not leave in my debt; he ran away in a very unbecoming manner, that is all. You must understand, sir——"

And then, by this time quite convinced that if ever there was a perfect gentleman that one now stood before her, she began the story of Mr. Dyot's strange flitting, and related it from first to last. She told him how the stout man with the walking-stick, and the little puckered-faced man in black, who looked like an undertaker, came first of all, and there was words between them; then, how that they went away, and the little puckered-faced man came again in the evening, bringing a woman with him; and then it was discovered that Mr. Dyot was gone, and the little man "went ferreting about the room, and poking and prying into corners and cupboards, and was in a terrible taking;" then, how that soon after they were gone, the stout, impudent man with the walking-stick came again, and in a very unpleasant manner declared that he would wait until Mr. Dyot returned, and that he sat down on the house-step with that intent, as she saw from the parlour window; and, furthermore, she informed the Lombard Street Turkey merchant that, as she still kept watch at the window, fearing that when her lodger did return there would be some sort of bother between him and the impudent stout man, a woman—not the woman that accompanied the little man with the puckered face, but quite a young thing—came along and spoke to the stout man on the steps, and seemed to know him, for, after a long whispering and crying, she thought if she might believe her ears, which were not so good as they used to be, the stout man and the young woman went off together. A most interesting narration, and one that the Turkey merchant listened to with an amount of attention that was not a whit affected.

"A bad lot altogether, evidently," he observed; "and have they been here since, ma'am?"

"Not one of them."

"Not the doc—— the dark man? Didn't you say that one was a dark man, ma'am?"

"A stout man, sir," returned the old

lady, mildly correcting him; "a stout man with a walking-stick and a very loud voice. How or why that Mr. Dyot escaped out of the window is a mystery to me."

"But you just now told me that the little man explained that it was a mistake about the door being locked on the inside," remarked the Turkey merchant, with an avidity that was convincing of the deep interest he took in the tale.

"So he said; but we afterwards found the catch broken."

Mr. Micah stepped out on to the balcony, and saw at once how easy it would be to escape that way if the tide was in and a boat engaged. He inquired of the old lady as to the condition of the tide on the evening in question, but she could give him no information; indeed, she had no more to tell than she had already told; discovering which, the Turkey merchant warmly shook hands with her and promised to call to-morrow and hear the result of her application to Bullion and Walmsley.

It was quite clear to Micah that Mr. Dyot, pressed by his enemies, had escaped by the balcony, sacrificing everything for the sake of his precious treasure, which, no doubt, he had carried off with him. Before the day was at an end, he had searched the almanack and found that at the time when the old lady's lodger had so mysteriously vanished, the tide was in.

For several days after this lucky day Micah Blake displayed curious affection for the society of watermen. He gossiped with them at their various plying-places; he was rowed up the river for the sake of being rowed down again! he took his ale and tobacco, of evenings, at water-side houses frequented by men who went down to the river in boats. He passed as a person that was addicted to wagering on races, and in that guise was committed to several rash though small bets.

He was successful at last, however—as he deserved to be, if patience is worthy of reward. It was at Queenhithe, and in the parlour of the "Skiff Aground" there. "Talking of queer fares," said a certain jolly young waterman whom the reader has met before, "talking of queer fares, Joe [this to a fellow watercraftsman], that was a queer one of mine from Stangate. Hang me if I don't think that the bums must have been on the stairs, judging from the skeered look of his face, ha! ha!"

"Three mile for half a guinea, wasn't it?" Joe remarked.

"Nigher four, Joe. No matter for that; damme, I'd ha' carried him for tuppence."

"How d'ye make it nigher four, Charley?" Joe asked. A very particular person as to details was Joe. "Bull Stairs, Rotherhithe, wasn't it, where you set him down?"

"Bull Stairs? Yes."

"Then that isn't more than three miles from the bridge at Westminster. I'll pound it. What do you say, mate?" This to Micah.

"Stangate he said, didn't he?" remarked the person in question, assuming an air of indifference. "What part of Stangate? That makes all the difference, you know."

"Just this side of the boatbuilder's," Charley explained.

"Ay, I know; there are some houses there, with balconies."

"The very identical," returned Charley. "It was from one of them balconies that he hailed me."

"Well, I should say that from there to Bull Stairs was as nigh to between three and four miles as possible."

"And nigher three than four," persisted Joe the waterman.

"Very likely; you ought to know."

"Anyhow, it was a queer sort of fare; and that was all I meant to say at first," observed Charley, in a conciliatory tone.

"So I say," and Micah emptied the jug that the waterman returned to him.

In less than an hour Mr. Micah Blake was at Bull Stairs, full of confidence as to the future. "The fact is," Micah shrewdly argued, "that old thief, Gurd, has stumped Dyot out of ready money, and he has come to this unfashionable part, where lodgings are cheap, and where nobody is likely to think of looking after such a respectable chap as he is, until he can conveniently dispose of part of his precious swag and take himself off to another country. I'll find him if he's to be found. If he sticks to his old plan of carrying his bag about with him, it will be an easy matter enough. He might as well pin a ticket on to his back or go about singing out, 'My name is Dyot: who wants me?'"

Nevertheless, the matter that seemed so easy was not quickly consummated. Day after day passed, until Micah's pocket grew alarmingly lean, and he was as far as ever. He began to despond. "P'r'aps he's ill," thought he; "there's no knowing. He's been pretty well worried and driven about lately. P'r'aps as soon as he got down here he was took ill, and is now lying at one of the lodging-houses here. Pretty dens they are! I wouldn't give much for his chance of getting well if once they got scent of what was in that leather bag. P'r'aps he has caught sight of me, instead of me catching sight of him, and has give me the slip. If he don't turn up by to-morrow, I shall have to give up the hunt; for one and tuppence is all I've got in the blessed world."

But once again his enduring patience was destined to reward. Each night of the five nights he had spent at Rotherhithe he had slept at a different lodging-house from the last, and this night he adopted the same plan. He had taken his ticket at the door (for which he paid fourpence halfpenny, that being the sum charged for a single-bedded room, and Micah inclined to ways of decency), and was proceeding to the common kitchen at the end of the passage, there to cook the frugal supper he had brought in with him, when suddenly his steps were arrested by the sound of a peculiar voice, and, turning about, lo! there, within twenty feet of him, was the person for whom he had so long and vainly sought.

Had he not have heard his voice, however, it is very doubtful if he would have known him; for, in place of a tall hat, he wore a broad-flapped cap of the wide-awake species which overhung his features considerably; and, though he carried a bag, it was not the leather one, but larger, and made out of some material such as dark serge.

"You can have the same room as last night, if you like it," he heard the hall-porter remark.

"That will do very well," Mr. Dyot replied.

"Number thirty-seven, I think; that's it. You're just in time: thirty-six was the last give out."

"Thanky. I'll go up to bed at once."

"All right; take a candle; you know the way."

And up-stairs he went, toiling slowly and painfully, like a man who has walked many miles.

Although hungry, for he had tasted no food since the morning, Mr. Micah Blake made but a poor supper that evening. The discovery he had so recently made, though he had so eagerly sought it and prayed that it might presently transpire, was altogether too much for him. It was disastrous to his cookery, and even had his appetite been in primest condition, it would scarcely have been tempted by the charred and overdone rasher set before it. He looked at his ticket and found that the number it bore was thirty-six. "It doesn't follow that it is next door to thirty-seven for all that," he reflected with satisfaction.

It did not follow that bed-room thirty-six should adjoin bed-room thirty-seven, for lodging-house keepers are proverbially erratic in their dormer arrangements; but in this instance the simple plan was adopted, and when the supperless rogue took his candle and stole up to bed, which was in a room at the very top of the house, there, within three feet of his own chamber-door was another plainly figured one higher. He glanced furtively through the keyhole and saw that all within was dark. Inside his own door there was a bolt as well as a lock, and the fair inference was that the door of thirty-seven was similarly secured.

"Phew! I wish that Teddy was here," softly whispered the coward; "it's more in his line than mine. I shall lose it now if I am not lucky."

Had he said if I am not plucky it would have nigher expressed his meaning; not that it mattered much, since sitting on a bed in the dark is not the way to cultivate either pluck or luck; and this is what Micah did hour after hour, except that after the house was quiet, at frequent intervals, he would steal out on to the landing and listen at the door of the room where unsuspecting Mr. Dyot was lying.

Towards daylight Micah had worked

himself into a state of feverish excitement. He felt that here was a chance that might never occur again, and which ought not to be allowed to slip by. But what was he to do? He had no tools to force a bolt or a lock, and to break in on the sleeper by putting his shoulder to the door was not to be for a moment thought of.

Casting about in an aimless despairing way, his eyes wandered to the chimney, which was of the ancient, capacious sort. This was more in his way. Stepping softly across the room, he put his head in at the sooty aperture, and discovered that within ten feet were the pot and the outlet, and that a man of his dimensions might climb through the space within with ease, and, by dislodging the pot, so reach the roof. "If Dyot's chimney is as convenient, I may make up for lost time, and have the laugh of Teddy yet." Micah chuckled, gleefully.

Buttoning his coat up to his chin, he courageously stepped up on to the fireplace hobs, and, once in for it, went at his work without scruple. The constantly-falling soot, and the rasping of his shins and knuckles against the rough, grimy bricks, rendered his ascent far from pleasant; but at length the chimney-pot was reached; and, with considerable difficulty, having but one hand to work with, he succeeded in wrenching it off, and next minute he stood out on the house roof.

"Now for the chimney of thirty-seven!" said Micah, a grin of triumph beaming on his sooty countenance. But here what he very naturally supposed to be a bit of splendid fortune happened to him. While cautiously stepping along in the twilight, he discovered a trap-door that, from its position, he knew must lead to room thirty-seven. Lying flat on his belly, he brought his ear to the boards, and, listening, distinctly heard sounds of a person sleeping beneath.

"It *is* the room, I suppose," thought he, quite in a perspiration at his wonderful luck. "It is easy to see, however; and that without danger."

So saying, he produced from his pocket a clasp-knife with a gimlet attached to it, and softly bored a hole in the trap and peeped through. What he discovered must have been of a rather exciting character, for his legs trembled so as he lay as to dislodge fragments of mortar from the dingy tiles, causing them to rattle down into the gutter.

"Lord send the trap isn't bolted!" was his earnest mental ejaculation. "I'd give ten pounds, if I had as much, to find that the trap was not bolted!"

Once more he inserted the gimlet and gently raised it. The trap was *not* bolted; it yielded fully half an inch.

But the rogue had to proceed with extreme caution. The sleeper lay almost immediately beneath, and the least noise—a sudden puff of cold air might wake him. A little at a time the trap was raised until he could grasp the edges of it, and then, without so much as a creak, he lifted it up and put it back on the roof. Luck upon luck! Immediately below was a table, and on the table the precious bag, released from its serge envelope.

Immediately below; but so far down! Had the ceiling been but a foot lower there would have been no difficulty in reaching down and securing the precious object; but that foot made all the difference. It would be necessary for him to thrust his body quite through, and to hang on with one hand and his feet above.

And this difficult feat he attempted, being spurred to prodigious effort by the prize at his finger-tips; and, of a surety, he would have succeeded but for a trifling accident. Mr. Dyot suddenly awoke to the appalling apparition of a face, black as that of the father of evil hovering above him spiderwise. At that lodging-house the candlesticks supplied to the lodgers were of solid iron, and made to last. One of these stood by Mr. Dyot's bed-side, and catching it up, he hurled it with all his might at the hanging face, that instantly changed from black to hideous red, and down came Micah, with a crash, to the ground.

END OF SECOND VOLUME.

HARRILD, PRINTER, LONDON.

CPSIA information can be obtained
at www.ICGtesting.com
Printed in the USA
LVHW090838250222
711993LV00002B/68

9 783752 564150